CLARY INGRAM

ISBN: 0615572340
ISBN 13: 9780615572345

Library of Congress Number: 2011963022

PROLOGUE

There isn't a feeling in the world as wonderful as completing four years of high school. I thought my turn would never come to go to my first prom, make the senior class trip to Cancún, and best of all — graduate. It was almost yesterday that I was a freshman trying to find my way around the halls of Southside High. Now my class has been handed the torch.

I've watched friends who graduated before me race across the stage to receive their diplomas as if they were running to claim a lottery prize. Now as I enter into my last year of high school, I understand their excitement. The only thing missing in my life is a boyfriend.

Almost four years have passed and no one has ever stepped to me or looked my way. I keep telling myself that guys are just intimidated by a strong-minded girl like me. But after a while that theory begins to wear out, and you start to second-guess yourself. I think I'm a cute girl and that's why I don't understand why guys at school never want to get with me. I mean, I have friends who aren't all that, and they all have someone to call their own.

For example, my best friend, Andrea, isn't the cutest sister in the world, but she has a boyfriend named Terrell Lewis who is the bomb. At times, I find myself wondering what a day in her shoes would be like. I'm sure it would be like heaven to walk around school with someone who is all that and a bag of chips.

I'm tired of being the oddball in the group, the only girl without a boyfriend, which is the reason I've adopted a totally different attitude and a new style this year. Instead of dedicating every second of the day to my books in order to maintain a 4.0 grade point average, I've decided to take more pride in my appearance. Now I let my hair hang loose, since it's grown an inch past my shoulders over the summer, which in my opinion makes me look more mature. I've excluded sweats, T-shirts, and sneakers from my wardrobe. And this summer I ran my butt off until I lost the extra fifteen pounds I'd tagged on from eating greasy fast food. My hips and thighs were starting to spread out of control. Now I'm back to my ideal weight of 120 pounds.

Tomorrow is the first day of school, and for the first time I'm excited. I used to dread the start of a new school year because of my acne. Now that I got it under control from using treatments, I feel more confident.

Sometimes I look at the girl in the mirror named Karla Johnson and ask myself if she's really the same person as freshman year. The answer is no because I think I've come a very long way. Sometimes I have my doubts, but I've learned to accept the fact that I may never look like the girls in the music videos. It doesn't matter, though, because I look like me — how I've always seen myself. I just hope someone else sees me too.

Tomorrow I plan on snatching somebody's attention with this cute little face.

1

My first day back to school was better than I'd hoped. Besides the same old faces I've looked at for too many years, I saw plenty of new cute guys. The only thing was, they were freshmen. It seemed like freshmen were always nice and sweet, but as soon as they got caught up with the wrong crowd, they became trifling. The freshmen boys turned into dogs, while the freshmen girls turned into tramps.

The highlight of my day was when I bumped into Terrell in the hallway. *He is just so sexy*, I thought the moment I'd seen his strong chocolate legs. As usual, he was with his boys: Desmond, Rodney, and Vince. Surprisingly, all eyes were on me, and I could tell they were feeling me. I felt like doing cartwheels in the middle of the hallway while Terrell bit down on his bottom lip, like he was yearning for a taste of my hips.

After school, my two best friends, Cammy and Andrea paid me a visit at home. We had a good ole time. There was always something to gossip about after the first day of school, like who's hot and who's not. We sat in the den for hours bugging out over the finest brothers at school while drinking Kool-Aid.

They agreed that Rashard was the bomb even though he was gangster. Cornrows and tattoos was his style. Although

Rashard acted thuggish, he was still fly to the bone. He was the prettiest thug we'd ever seen. He had caramel-colored skin, hazel eyes, and nice thick lips. Rashard was from Brooklyn and he had the style and accent to prove it. He had a hard time fitting in when he transferred to Southside High. Everybody thought he was on drugs. He used to walk around school dressed in baggy clothing, a bandana tied around his head, rapping and barking like DMX. But everybody's perception of him changed when the varsity basketball coach molded his slim, 6'5" frame into balling material. He's led the county in scoring since he was a sophomore, and I'd be surprised if he didn't enter the upcoming NBA draft when he was the next best thing to Lebron James. Unfortunately, there was a rumor that Rashard only dated thick Latina girls, which was the reason I'd never paid attention to him.

If I had to take my pick for the most-finest boy at school — Terrell Lewis was the cream of the crop. He was the baddest brother that ever walked the face of the earth, except for my favorite singer, Usher. Terrell had smooth chocolate skin, a beautiful Colgate smile, and a banging body. To top the list, he always looked fly — unlike most of the nappy-headed boys who walked around school with their pants sagging off their butts. I'll never forget the time he took off his shirt during a football pep rally. I almost lost my mind when I saw his six-pack. Ever since that day, I've been dreaming of giving him a hot-oil body massage.

I'd had a crush on Terrell since middle school. I was the only one who liked him despite the fact he lived in the projects. Terrell would come to school in dingy clothes and holes in his shoes. Sometimes he'd wear the same thing three times a week, but I still thought he was handsome. Girls would turn their noses up at him because he couldn't afford designer clothes and brand-name shoes. When we got to high school, it was a different story. Once he made the football squad, all the girls hopped on his jock — especially my best friend, Andrea. She knew I liked him first but that never stopped her from approaching him. At one point in time, Andrea only liked white boys, but things had changed.

I felt guilty for allowing sinful thoughts of Terrell in my mind, although Andrea was busy lusting after Rashard. I doubt she realized that she had the perfect boyfriend. He was smart, funny, good-looking, and going places in life.

Andrea and Terrell had been together since freshman year, and they'd probably end up getting married if her daddy had anything to do with it. Andrea's daddy was a minister and he was strict. He made sure she was in church every Saturday and at Bible study six days a week, and the closest thing she got to recreation was choir rehearsal.

At times, I didn't understand what Terrell saw in Andrea. Personally, I didn't think she looked as good as me. Her skin was beige, needing a tan; she was bony and her hair was never done. On top of that, her wardrobe was busted. And last but not least, she was too bossy and judgmental. She expected everyone to be the perfect Christian like her. But overall she was a good friend, and every time I'd put her down, I felt guilty.

Cammy added my 18-year-old brother, Eric, to her mostfinest list. *She has gotta be kidding*, I thought. I knew I had put too much sugar in her Kool-Aid because she was acting dizzy. Then Andrea agreed that my brother was the bomb.

"Stop the madness," I said, lock-jawed from the sweetness of the Kool-Aid.

"Your brother looks like Bow Wow," Cammy said.

"Yeah, he sho nuff do," Andrea nodded.

"No, he doesn't."

"You need glasses," Cammy said.

"Don't fall for looks because he's a dog," I said.

"I don't care — he's gorgeous," she said.

I got jealous because Eric always received compliments. My brother was blessed with flawless brown skin and soft curly hair, but I didn't think he was the bomb. When he started treating girls with respect then he may've received my vote. Until then, he was an ugly person.

"Who do you consider fine then, Miss Karla?" Cammy said, eyeing me.

Andrea stared at me too.

I wouldn't have dared said Terrell so I blurted out, "Usher."

They laughed at me.

Cammy shook her head. "Keep dreaming, honey. That's Chilli's man."

I rolled my eyes at her. "You never know what the future may have in store for me."

We started cleaning up when we heard someone walk through the front door. I knew it was Mommy when I heard her high heels tap across the foyer. She said hello to us as she handed me my mail. Then she headed into her bedroom. I got nervous when I saw that it was my test scores. Cammy and Andrea had already received their ACT scores, which were high enough to get into Spelman. I was the only nervous soul left.

I handed my mail to Andrea to open and then closed my eyes.

"Before I open this envelope," she said, "I just wanna say there's always community college to consider if —"

"Will you open the damn letter before I slap you," Cammy interrupted.

Andrea rolled her eyes. "I'm trying to tell my friend that it's not the end of the world if she didn't do well."

My heart started pounding in my chest when I heard her trying to unseal the envelope. I said a quick prayer and squeezed my eyes closed tighter. I couldn't stand the thought of not being able to get into the college of my choice. I opened my eyes when I heard her fumbling with the envelope. Andrea seemed more nervous than I did.

Cammy snatched the envelope from her hands. "Let me do this," she said, ripping it open. The look on her face gave it away. "Girl, you knocked it out with a composite score of 28!" she screamed. "Spelman here we come, goddamnit!"

We hopped up and started jumping around like we'd lost our minds. I couldn't wait to tell Daddy the good news when he walked through the door. I was hoping to God he'd get me a brand-new Honda Civic like he'd been promising to do for the longest time. Plus, I'd been patient ever since he bought Eric a hoopdie for his birthday a year ago. I assumed my chances were good, especially since Daddy had received his long awaited promotion as Chief of Police.

It was getting late but we started making plans for life after graduation. We marked up our calendars, trying to figure out how many days we had left. We'd calculated 188 school days. It seemed like forever when I thought about it. We went around in a circle asking each other about majors. Andrea and I laughed when Cammy said she wanted to major in journalism so she could be seen on television every day, looking ghetto-fabulous. Although Andrea said she planned on getting her degree in psychology, her dream was to improve her vocals so she could tour with Kirk Franklin & the Family. As for me, I told them I wanted to major in English so I could be a professor at a historically black college like Spelman.

⌘ ⌘ ⌘

That night, I shoved my test scores into Daddy's face. I almost hit the roof when he told me I could get the Civic for my birthday next month. The thought of no longer having to catch the bus or depend on my friends for a ride had me excited. There was no way I could keep the news to myself. I went to my room and called my girls on three-way. When I told them the news, they screamed through the phone in excitement. As we sat on the phone chatting, I started flipping through last year's yearbook. I thought the pictures of me were awful. I was cursed my first year of high school. I used to be flat-chested and shapeless, then it seemed like one day the sun shined on me, ripening my breasts and curves. I couldn't believe how horrible my skin looked and now it was as smooth and pretty as a mango.

I flipped past a picture of Cammy and me standing side-by-side. She's always had it going on. In middle school, she had breasts and hips before everybody else. She even got her period early. I used to wish I could be like Cammy because all the guys dug her. She had beautiful cocoa-brown skin and long weave, which flowed down her back like Pocahontas. Her small waist-line and big booty attracted all the boys. She was a jazzy girl. The girl never got caught slipping when it came to clothes, jewelry, manicures, and hair. Her only flaw was her mouth, which never closed. She definitely deserved her nickname, Mouth Almighty. I was convinced that she got her outspokenness from her mom who was a local politician with a big voice in the black community.

I flipped to the next page and saw Terrell posing with his boys from the football squad. He had his arms folded, legs spread apart, and a mean mug on his face like he was letting the world know that he was on top of his game. He sure was too. Terrell rarely dropped a pass thrown his way and he had blazing speed. The boy was good — so good that he ranked number one on the list of top 100 high school players in the nation. Even though he missed the end of last season with a broken arm, he still sat atop the list for recruits. After he got hurt, the season went down the drain. Every week I had to deal with Eric's nasty attitude because they couldn't win a game. Last year was the first time in four years that our football team missed the playoffs. I knew this year would be different with Terrell coming back. This year, I planned on attending all of his games. I wouldn't have missed seeing him back in action for the world.

After I got off the phone, I tossed my yearbook to the side and lay in bed, thinking about Terrell for the rest of the night.

⌘　⌘　⌘

Football season was in progress. The school's atmosphere was no longer dead; school spirit was off the charts. Posters and banners hung in the hallways and everybody was fired up. Our first game was a week away against our rivals, the Tigers. Last year, they beat us silly in a game that was supposed to be a tribute to Coach Graham, who had lost his fight to prostate cancer during the middle of the year. Eric took the loss to heart because Coach Graham meant everything to him. He was the type of coach who actually cared about his players. His motto was "No Grades, No Football." Most of the team maintained a B average or better after he'd benched Eric during state's two years ago. Since then, Eric's been serious about education. He was retained his sophomore year, but finally that poor child was back on the right track.

One day after school, Andrea and I stayed to watch the boys' football practice. It was so hot that the steel bleachers roasted our thighs. I felt sorry for the players who looked drained. Despite the blistering heat, we enjoyed the action on the field. I couldn't keep my eyes off Terrell. On one play, he stretched high and snatched the ball out of midair.

"Good catch! That's how you stretch a defense!" one of the coaches shouted.

I was excited to see Terrell back in action after he was intentionally injured in last year's rivalry game. I bet that was a game Terrell wished he'd kept his mouth shut instead of talking smack.

"That's it, baby!" Andrea clapped as he fought for extra yardage after the catch.

Why was I jealous? Then the reality struck me that she had something I could never have — Terrell.

As he was tackled to the ground, my attention shifted to Eric. He'd collapsed in the middle of the field. I started to run out on the field until Andrea held me back.

All the coaches ran on the field. My brother wasn't moving; he was as stiff as a doorknob. I started crying.

"Call 911!" one of the athletic trainers shouted.

Within minutes, we heard sirens. Moments later, Andrea tried to calm me down as we stood in the bleachers watching Eric being hauled off the field on a stretcher. I was hysterical.

The coaches wrapped up practice for the day. Andrea and I waited for Terrell to change. I thought I was going to have a nervous breakdown while we stood outside of the locker room waiting to go to the hospital. When Terrell rushed out of the locker room shirtless, I got sidetracked, as I watched him slide a T-shirt over his chest. He smelled like he'd missed a shower, but it didn't faze me one bit. After Terrell put on his shirt, he wrapped his arm around my shoulders and squeezed me. "Don't worry, okay?" he said.

Andrea looked as if she was jealous, but I didn't sweat it.

"Okay," I nodded. It was hard for me to take Terrell's advice when a player from Miami High had died last week of heat stroke while at practice.

"He probably got a li'l dehydrated, but that happens sometimes," he reassured me.

I felt confident while he cuddled me in his strong arms. A second later, he handed me a clean towel out of his book-bag.

I wiped the tears from my face and said, "Thank you."

"No problem."

It felt so good to have him by my side.

⌘　⌘　⌘

We drove to a total of five hospitals after receiving the wrong information from faculty at school. Unfortunately, there was still no trace of Eric. By the time the sun had gone down, we were still clueless. I'd tried calling Mommy and Daddy, but they were nowhere to be found. My head was throbbing in pain. I began to think the worst, like my brother could've been toe tagged and shoved into a freezer.

Finally, Andrea dropped me off at home. She and Terrell offered to keep me company, but I told them no thank you because they'd already done enough.

"Are you sure, Karla?" Andrea said.

I smiled even though I was sad. "I'll be fine."

"Everything's gonna be a'ight," Terrell said. "Eric's probably over a chick's house laying pipe."

"You need to watch your mouth," Andrea scolded him.

"It's true," he said. "Y'all don't know him like I do."

I got out of the car while Andrea started preaching.

"You have no respect," she said.

"Whatever. Why you trippin'?" he said. They started arguing.

"I'll see you guys later." I walked away feeling down and out.

When I went inside of the house, it was pitch dark. I turned on the lights and saw a note sitting on the front room coffee table that read: "Me and your mama will be back late tonight so if there's an emergency call Officer Jackson. Love, Daddy."

I was tempted to call Daddy's cell phone, but I didn't want to ruin their night out. I sat on the couch worried to death; the sight of Eric's body falling limp on the football field was stuck in my mind. My eyes started watering. I almost gave in and called Daddy until I heard noises coming from my bedroom. I tiptoed down the hallway and peeked inside my room. Clothes were on the floor and my bed was rocking. I couldn't believe my eyes; Eric had a girl in my canopy bed. The girl was bent over on her knees, while Eric was pumping her from behind.

I barged into the room. They both looked shocked to see me as they covered themselves up in shame. I was shocked, too, when I saw who the tramp was in my bed.

"Cammy!" I yelled.

I thought we were friends; we practically told each other everything. I guess everything except the fact she was giving it up to Eric. We were all supposed to keep our virginities until we got married. She lied to Andrea and me. There we were thinking that we were the last virgins left at school. I should've known it was too good to be true.

"We weren't doing nothin'," Eric said, reaching to the floor for his boxer shorts.

"Do I look like a fool to you?" I said.

Cammy looked embarrassed as she tried fixing her weave.

"Get your clothes and get out of my house, bitch!" I yelled at her.

She stomped her way into the bathroom, wrapped in my Sponge Bob sheets, and slammed the door. I couldn't believe she had the nerve to catch an attitude. I looked at Eric disgusted. "Why my room of all places?"

He shrugged. "She was waiting on you then one thing led to another."

"That's no excuse for you to be so inconsiderate of my property. You can keep those nasty sheets," I said, flipping mad. "We were worried sick about you while you were in here humping."

"My body was dehydrated."

"So I guess you feel better now, huh?"

He smiled. "A brother feels deeply replenished. She got da bomb!"

"You nasty dog. Let's see how replenished you feel when I tell Mommy what you were doing in her house. The nerve of that skank doing you in my damn bed!" I felt sick.

"Will you calm down? What's the big deal?"

"You don't have any morals or respect for your body, so I wouldn't expect you to understand."

"Understand what?"

"We were supposed to keep our virginity till marriage," I said, feeling betrayed.

"Yeah right. Cammy is a straight freak. If you don't know, you better ask somebody."

I didn't know which was worse: finding my brother having sex in my bed, or finding out that my best friend had been lying to me. "I hope to God you used a condom because if the skank ends up pregnant that's on you!"

"Yes, we did use a condom, Mother," he said, holding up an empty Trojan wrapper.

"So disgusting."

A couple of minutes later, Cammy came out of the bathroom, dressed. She tried talking to me, but I didn't care to hear it. I didn't have anything to say to her. I made her get out of my house. She didn't have any respect for our home anyway. If her name spread around school like a bad case of measles, she had no one to blame but herself. I hoped she didn't expect to cry on my shoulder when her name got run through the dirt. I thought it would've suited her just right for lying.

After busting them having sex, I couldn't wait to tell Andrea. She was going to die. After I changed the sheets and disinfected my room with Lysol, I picked up the house phone. I was so anxious to spread the gossip that I'd dialed the wrong number two times. Finally, I heard Andrea's voice on my third try. "You won't believe what I have to tell you," I said.

"What is it?"

"You won't believe it!"

"All right, all right. Will you spill the beans?"

"Okay, get a grip. If you're sitting down hold onto your chair, girly."

She sucked her teeth. "What is it already?"

I told her that I'd caught Eric and Cammy hunching in my bed.

"*Are you serious?*"

"She let him do her doggy style."

"What!"

"I'm as shocked as you are. She said he was the bomb, but I didn't think she'd let him rock her world."

"She could've had me fooled."

"Me too!"

Andrea and I gossiped about Cammy all night. We couldn't believe she had given up her goodies. Word from Eric after she left, was that she'd been giving it up since 8th grade, which classified her as an *undercover ho*. If it was actually true, and Eric wasn't making it up, then her parents needed to beat her behind like a runaway slave. I hoped my brother was playing when he gave me the 411.

As I lay in bed, I put Andrea on hold while I checked to see who was calling the other line. It was Terrell asking for me. My heart began to race. It was beating so fast that I could've had a heart attack. I took a deep breath and told him to hold on. My hands were trembling as I clicked over to the other line. *The day can't possibly end better than this*, I thought. I let Andrea know quickly I'd talk to her tomorrow.

"Goodness, girl," she said. "Who is it on the other line that got you so excited?"

"Nobody, bye."

After I clicked her off the line, it wasn't surprising to hear the first sentence to leave Terrell's mouth: "I told you your brother was a player." He laughed. "Eric told me that he smashed that ass from every angle."

I shook my head because that was exactly how reputations got ruined. Cammy was in for it.

After Terrell got the excitement out of his system, we talked about life and we shared fond memories of taking the same classes together freshman year. Our three-hour conversation was flowing so well that I hadn't realized it was going on midnight. Things took off on a personal route when Terrell asked me if I would be interested in him if he were single. Just then, I heard my daddy say, "No." Then he told me to get off the phone.

I had no idea that he was home, let alone eavesdropping. I was so embarrassed.

2

Tonight we'd play the Tigers at their stadium. I sat in class distracted because I didn't have anybody to go with me to the game. I would've never imagined I'd have this dilemma on my birthday. Andrea's daddy wouldn't let her go because she had district choir rehearsal, and me going with Cammy was completely out of the question. I refused to hang with her. I didn't want her to ruin my reputation like she'd already ruined hers. I'd rather go to the game alone than be caught anywhere with her. She already knew that sexing a guy on the football team was equivalent to suicide. Any girl in her right mind would've rather been dead instead of talked about like a dog inside of the boy's locker room.

After class, I met Andrea for the pep rally. I wasn't the only one excited about the game — the entire school was crunk. The gym was rocking while the cheerleaders bounced to the music with their pom-poms. Some students came to school rocking the team's colors to show their school spirit. I did too. Girls were eyeballing me because I had on Eric's jersey. I thought it was hilarious.

As I watched the cheerleaders do their chitty-chitty-bang-bang routine, my attention drifted. I heard the football team shouting in the hallway, preparing to make their entrance. My heart anticipated Terrell's introduction.

After the cheerleaders finished their routine, the football team burst into the gym while "Lose Yourself" by Eminem played in the background. Everybody went mad. The white kids standing beside Andrea and me scared us as they stomped in the bleachers like crazies. The trembling bleachers felt like they were going to collapse.

The place erupted when Terrell spoke into the microphone, announcing he'd be playing in tonight's big game. My cheeks were jittering as I held back my emotions while he spoke.

"This is my last year!" he added. "And I'm gon' make sure we turn this motherfucker out!"

Our principal, Mr. Jones, snatched the microphone out of Terrell's hand, giving him an evil stare. I thought the place was going to crumble to the ground. Luckily, security escorted most of the idiots who were causing chaos out of the gym before somebody ended up hurt.

After all the commotion, I thought we'd better win tonight instead of getting our tails beat like last year. We played so horrible that I was afraid to wear my Bucks jacket in public. I'd already made up my mind that I was going to the game even if I had to hitchhike. I wouldn't have missed Terrell's first game back for the world. And most important of all, it was the first game without my folks coming along to cramp my style.

During lunchtime, Andrea and I sat away from Cammy. Every day, it felt weird seeing her at a different table than us, sitting with other people. After her sexcapade with Eric two weeks ago, we were no longer friends.

Cammy and I caught each other's eye. She was looking at me as if she had a lot to say. Every time I looked at her face, I visualized her bent over, breasts wobbling, taking it from the back.

I looked back down and started eating the cafeteria's nasty meatloaf. The FDA needed to have the cafeteria ladies arrested for feeding us this garbage. I spat out the mushy half-cooked meat and threw all my food in the garbage. Thankfully, Andrea had cheese crackers for me to snack on because my stomach was growling.

Terrell walked into the cafeteria with a newspaper nudged underneath his arm. He had on a red shirt and a pair of baggy blue jeans. I smiled inside because he looked scrumptious in red. He skipped the long line, paid for his food, and then sat at our table. Andrea kissed him on the cheek.

"Happy birthday!" he said, looking at me.

I smiled. "Thank you."

When I'd talked to Terrell over the phone, he'd made it clear that he wasn't happy. After he gave me the scoop, I learned that things weren't always as they seemed, although Andrea fronted like her relationship was a bed of roses. Terrell told me that the two of them together were like oil and water — they didn't mix. He claimed she had taken religion to the extreme and it was taking a toll on their relationship. He didn't come outright and say it, but he'd hinted that she wasn't giving up the goodies. I didn't know why he expected anything different when Andrea lived the Bible.

Terrell started eating his meatloaf. "Are you gonna be able to make it to my game tonight?" he asked Andrea. "I need your support."

"You know I have choir rehearsal tonight," she said.

"So I take it choir rehearsal is more important than your man?"

"We've been through this time and time again, Terrell. God comes first in my life. You know that."

"Yeah, whatever," he said, grubbing on the meatloaf. "This is the biggest game of the season."

"Nothing is bigger than God," she replied.

Terrell looked mad. "I'm not tryin' to lead you astray, damn. All I want you to do is come watch me ball."

Andrea put on her holier-than-thou face. "The bishop at my church said we're living in the last days and we must —"

Terrell plugged his fingers inside his ears. "I don't wanna hear what the bishop said."

"Well, it's better you hear it now than on Judgment Day. 'Every knee shall bow and every tongue shall confess that —'"

"I can't take this girl, yo!"

"Well, pardon me for trying to save your lost soul. You can go to hell for all I care." She went back to chomping on her tuna salad.

Terrell took a peek at the newspaper and shook his head. "These cats actually think they can play man-to-man coverage and stop me. Big joke." He nodded. "I'm gon' be off the hinges tonight!"

"I wish I could be there to watch you play," Andrea said.

"You just pray them fools don't try to take any cheap shots at my knees." He crumpled up the newspaper.

"I'll pray for you."

"Nah, you better pray I don't catch a charge for whoopin' somebody's ass out there tonight," Terrell said, looking hard. He took one last bite of his meatloaf and dumped it into the garbage can. "I'm goin' to Mickey D's to get some real grub."

Andrea scrambled to pack up her things. "Wait for me, pooky," she said.

Terrell looked at me and said, "Are you comin' wit' us?"

I wanted to say yes, but I was sure Andrea didn't want me trailing behind her and her man all the time. "No, thank you. You two go ahead," I said.

"Are you sure?"

I nodded.

"A'ight then," he shrugged.

"Toodles," Andrea said.

⌘　⌘　⌘

After they left, Cammy kept staring at me. She was annoying me to the point I felt like walking out of the cafeteria. All of a sudden, she stood up and walked towards me. She sat at my table, but I acted like she was invisible. Not before I'd gotten a good look at her, though. This was the second time she'd come to school with hickeys all over her neck. The girl had no shame.

"Karla," she said.

I refused to talk to her lying ass.

Cammy began to annoy me as she called my name. "Karla," she repeated.

"What?" I finally said.

"Why are you and Andrea acting so funny towards me?"

I couldn't believe my ears. "It should be obvious."

"What's the big deal?" Cammy shrugged, looking confused. "We're all adults."

"The big deal is that you lied. We're supposed to be better than that."

"I was scared."

"Scared of what?"

"What y'all would think of me if y'all knew I was getting down like that."

"Since eighth grade, Cammy?" I said, shaking my head. "And you couldn't tell me? Our friendship is supposed to go beyond anything."

She could barely look me in the eye. "Then will you forgive me?"

I felt like I shouldn't have forgiven her for breaking our trust, but then I thought to myself, *Nobody's perfect.* "On two conditions," I said.

"What?"

"That there'll be no more keeping secrets . . . and that you'll bring your hot butt to the game with me tonight."

"Done deal. And happy birthday, friend." She reached across the table and hugged me tight. "I miss you guys."

I hugged her back, glad in a way that we were cool again. I'd missed her too.

She grinned. "Guess what?"

"What?"

"Rashard asked about you."

My eyes popped wide open. "Stop lying! You're just trying to make me feel good," I said, blushing.

"I gave him your phone number."

I was overjoyed. "You did! When? And why hasn't he called?"

"Hold on to your panties. I just gave him your digits today."

I gave her high five. "Good looking out — but wait a minute, why couldn't he approach me like a real man? We aren't in middle school, hellooo."

"Does it matter, heffa? He's feeling you! That's the only thing that counts."

I was thrilled, but then I felt awkward about it. "But why me? I'm not exactly his type; he likes big-booty Spanish girls."

"Stop being so hard on yourself, Karla. If you don't think you're the bomb, then nobody else will either." Cammy was fussing with her top, trying to hide the deep-red hickeys on her neck. She must've not known I'd already peeped them out.

"Can I ask you something?" I said.

"Go ahead."

I paused. I was kind of scared, especially when she stared at me like she was anxious to answer.

"Come on, let it out."

How is it? I wanted to ask.

"Let it out, girl, or forever hold your peace."

"Never mind," I blushed. My question had to wait till I was more comfortable.

Cammy grabbed my hand over the table. "Look who just walked in the cafeteria!"

"Who?" I said, afraid to look.

"Mr. Bling-Bling himself." She nodded like she was amazed.

I turned and looked. Rashard and his clique were at the door. "He is the bomb," I sighed.

"Yes he is, girl, with his sexy self. You better get to work on him before I do," she said, popping her cherry-red lips.

Rashard looked like a diamond showcase. Everyone thought he was illegally accepting money from an agent. I didn't doubt it either. Every day the boy rolled to school in a Range Rover with 24-inch rims. Not to mention, he wore more jewels than Li'l Wayne. I hoped he was smart enough to invest his money instead of wasting it away on material things.

"He's coming this way," Cammy said.

"Oh my goodness! How do I look, girl?" I fussed with my hair and pulled my shirt to where it was supposed to lay.

"Calm down, you look cute."

Rashard stopped at our table and flashed us a cute grin. "How are you ladies doing?" he said all smooth and whatnot.

"Fine, thank you very much," Cammy said, begging for attention. His sparkly diamond-encrusted medallion had her in a trance.

Rashard set his gorgeous eyes on me, ignoring Cammy. "Whaddup, mami?" he said to me.

I was a nervous wreck as I watched his tongue glide across his gorgeous thick lips. "Hi."

"You don't mind if I hit you up sometime, do you?"

I smiled shyly. "Not at all."

"I had to come over here and make sure it was all right with you. I would hate for you to assume I'm not man enough for you, shorty."

As soon as he walked away, Cammy looked at me. "See, I told you!" she said excitedly. "Did you see the ice on his neck? Cha-ching. You've hit the jackpot, girl!"

I was still in denial as I watched him leave the cafeteria.

⌘　⌘　⌘

That night before the game, Cammy swore she was allowed to use her folks' car while they were in Vegas enjoying their twentieth anniversary. I refused to believe Cammy's parents left her the keys to their brand-new convertible Jag while they were out of town. I was hesitant to get in the car because she drove too fast and too crazy. I looked at my brother's raggedy pickup sitting in the yard. "Let's take Eric's truck," I said.

"Are you crazy? Rule number one: If you want a baller, then you *gots* ta ride like a baller."

"A baller?" I said, uninterested in her reasoning for taking her mother's car. Cammy's mother was a big woman and she didn't play.

"Yeah, a player with some cheese, act like you know," she said, cranking up the car. She threw on her shades and then let back the top on the convertible. "Let's go, chile."

I hopped in the car like a fool.

On the way to the game, Cammy had "This is How We Do" by G-Unit blaring through the speakers. Cute guys broke their necks to look at us, while our hair blew in the wind and our skin glowed in the sunset. Cammy's cute face and fresh hairdo had them honking their horns. Although my hair wasn't as cute as hers, I still caught a few glimpses. Suddenly, I didn't feel bad about taking her mother's car after all.

When we got to the stadium, we couldn't find anywhere to sit down; there wasn't an empty seat in the house. Thanks to Cammy, we'd missed the first quarter because she had to hang outside the stadium and talk with her other friends. As we searched for seats, Terrell's clique spotted us and made room for us in their section. Rodney and Desmond recapped the game for us. They said Eric had the hot hand. He'd completed five of eight passes and thrown for two touchdowns. Terrell, on the flipside, had three catches for a total of thirty yards and was done for the night. He'd gone out of the game with a sprained ankle in the first quarter.

"My dawg just can't find a way to stay healthy," Rodney said, shaking his head pitifully.

The entire second half, I watched Terrell limp down the sidelines pumping up the team. We were ahead 21-3. By the fourth quarter, we'd let the Tigers back into the game. With the score close at 21-20, Eric looked determined not to let the game slip away. On third down, he snuck out of the pocket and scrambled down the field. Eric was known for his quick feet like Michael Vick. Everyone jumped to their feet when he dove into the end zone. The noise level of the crowd sent chills down my spine as they cheered for Eric.

After the field goal, we went up eight points, and it was game over. Eric took off his helmet and held it to the sky after we kicked butt. Everybody in the stands started chanting, "*Uh uh uh uh oh!*"

Cammy stood up and clapped for Eric like he was her prized possession. I doubt she'd be cheering for him if she knew he was a straight dog.

After the game, Eric chased us down and tongue-tied Cammy in front of all the cheerleaders. He had to be serious about her to take it to that extent. Usually, my brother wouldn't have done anything to jeopardize his so-called game. Even the cheerleaders looked shocked.

While Cammy and Eric were sucking face, I walked to the other end of the stadium to be nosy. Terrell was holding conversation with a couple of guys on the opposite team. They were laughing and joking while standing on the track.

I turned around when someone tapped my shoulder. It was Hollis, the drum major who'd mastered every instrument in the band. He may've been able to play every musical tune to life, but when it came to fresh breath, he didn't know the key. He began playing "A Ribbon in the Sky" by Stevie Wonder on his flute. It sounded good but I wanted to push his tall lanky body over the railing for blocking my view of Terrell. Every time I saw Hollis, he reminded me of Bobby Brown with his Gumby high-top fade.

"Hollis, can you please move out of the way? I can't see," I said, standing on my tiptoes.

"Excuse me then." He packed away his flute. "You'll learn how to appreciate the art of music one day."

"Well until that day comes, please move," I said, fanning him away.

Hollis found my focus of attention and sucked his teeth. "Y'all girls are so dumb. Y'all will pass up on a good brother like me because I don't play ball."

"And what is your point?"

He got mad. "I hope he breaks your heart."

"Whatever, you better move before I slap you."

"You're just like the rest," he mumbled, walking away.

Terrell took off his jersey and shoulder pads. My eyes almost popped out of my head. He had on a tank top, which made his shoulders look pleasing. He was grimacing in pain while the trainer un-taped his ankle. When Terrell turned his body, I got a perfect view of him. He took off his tank top and started flexing his chest muscles, as if he knew I was admiring him from afar. Although he deserved applause for a banging body, I walked away. I refused to fall into a deep sea of lustful thoughts.

As I headed the opposite way, I had to look at Cammy and Eric. They were wrapped in each other's arms. I suddenly felt lonely — everybody had a special someone except for me. I was tired of seeing painted pictures of other people in love. I was ready to go home and cuddle up under my sheets. After all, I probably would've had a better chance of getting the guy that I wanted in my dreams.

I went and stood next to Cammy. She and Eric were all over each other. My brother had his hands gripped on her booty. I sucked my teeth while they kissed. "Cammy, are you ready to go?"

She ignored me.

"All that garbage isn't necessary in public," I said.

"You'll learn how it goes one day," Eric said, wiping slobber from his lips.

"Oh shut up."

"Maybe if you had a boyfriend, you wouldn't be so grouchy all the time," he said.

"Cammy, if this is the kind of abuse I gotta take for the rest of the night, can you please take me home?"

"Karla, it's only 9:30. The night's just beginning," she said.

"I don't care; just take me home."

Cammy sucked her teeth. "I don't see why you let him upset you."

"Go ahead and take her home so we can do our thing," Eric said, rubbing her hips. "I wanna see you work it tonight."

She smiled. "Oh you do?"

I could've vomited. "Please stop."

"My little sister got a curfew to beat," he said. "I tell you what, drop her off at home and we'll chill at T's crib. You dig?"

"Hell no, I ain't taking my mama's car over in that crack-head neighborhood."

"Girl, come on now, stop tripping."

As soon as Terrell's name was mentioned, my plans changed. I longed for the moment to be in his company. "It's my birthday," I butted in. "I can stay out late tonight. Where are y'all going?"

"Oh it is your birthday. Happy birthday — I forgot," Eric said, hugging me.

I pushed him away. "Boy, you stink. What are y'all doing tonight?"

"I wish I was doing her," he said, tapping Cammy on the rear.

She smiled. "Cut it out."

I rolled my eyes. "Y'all getting on my nerves with that crap."

"So go home," he said.

"No," I said.

Cammy grabbed Eric to the side and whispered something in his ear.

I folded my arms. "If y'all don't want me to go, just say it."

Cammy looked at me and smiled. "You know we love you."

"Sure, my own brother didn't even remember my birthday," I said, walking away.

⌘   ⌘   ⌘

Later that night we drove over to Terrell's crib. He lived in Liberty Square — the most crime-infested public housing apartment complex in Miami. As we rode through the apartment complex in Cammy's mother's brand-new Jaguar, she was paranoid. I was on edge, too, with all the criminal activity going on. We saw a crackhead wheeling a 52-inch TV across the street in a grocery basket, a prostitute giving head, and a dude smoking crack. The level of ignorance and poverty was hard to believe.

After circling the building five times, we found Terrell's apartment. The numbering of the apartments was confusing. Cammy blew the horn like a mad woman.

Eric and Terrell came outside. I fixed my hair as Terrell walked towards the car. I made sure there wasn't a strand out of place.

Eric opened my door and said, "Hit the back, shawty."

I got in the back seat without making fuss; he was lucky I was in a good mood. As Terrell got in the car beside me, I looked him over closely. He was dressed to impress; he had on a black V-neck shirt and a pair of matching jeans. He rested his arm across the back seat and I could smell his Sean John cologne, which made me melt.

"'Ey y'all, what it do?" he said, rubbing his hand across the leather seats. "This is a tight ride, Cammy."

"Thank you, boo," she said.

"I might have to cop me one of these bad babies when I get to the NFL," Eric said, checking out the car.

"Not before you buy me a Benz," Cammy said.

I rolled my eyes to the sky because Cammy was such a gold digger.

As we rode the highway, Eric's hand rode up Cammy's leg. I tapped his headrest when we almost swerved into another lane. "Let her drive, idiot!" I said.

"Shut up and mind your own business," Eric said.

"Pardon me but I'm not trying to die!"

I noticed Terrell was as quiet as a mouse. He stared off into space as if he were lost. I started to strike up a conversation when his cell phone rang. "Everybody, Andrea said hello," he said. Then he started grinning and whispering.

Something told me to go home. I think I would've had more fun listening to my mother complain about the kids at her school who couldn't read but could recite all the rap songs on the radio.

We stopped at Cammy's house. "What are we doing?" Eric said.

"I think I may've left the front door unlocked," Cammy said.

We saw someone run across her yard dressed in a black hoodie.

"What in the world was that thing?" she said.

"I don't know and I'm not trying to find out," Eric said.

"Please don't tell me one of those crackheads followed us," I sighed.

Cammy quickly let down the top on the convertible.

Eric looked at Terrell. "Did you see that, dawg?" he said.

"See what?"

"Get off the phone, man."

"A'ight, hold on for a minute," he said, putting his ear back to the phone. "I'll holler at you later. I love you too," he whispered. Terrell lifted up one hand, as if they were praying.

"She got T on lock and he ain't even get the draws yet," Eric nodded.

"Shoosh, have some respect!" I said, spraying everyone mistakenly.

Eric wiped off his forehead. "Damn, girl, calm down."

Cammy was about to pop as she held back her laughter.

"Amen," Terrell said. Then he looked at us. "Man, y'all are triflin'," he said, hanging up.

"Since the Lord got your back," Eric said, "why don't you get out and see what ran in the backyard?"

"Nobody gets out of the car. Let's call the police," I said.

"We don't need no police when there's two gangsters in the car. Ain't that's right, dawg?" Terrell said, expecting Eric to co-sign.

"Huh?" Eric said.

Terrell sucked his teeth. "Forget you, dawg. I ain't no punk."

I grabbed his shirttail. "Terrell, call the police — they might have a gun."

"Baby, wit' all these muscles, I'm bulletproof."

"I have a feeling you're gonna be sorry if you get outta this car," Cammy said, sounding spooky.

Terrell hobbled out of the car with his sore ankle like an idiot. Eric followed him. I thought my brother had better sense. I crossed my fingers as they crossed the yard. They went into the backyard and never came back. I began to worry.

After five minutes, Cammy suggested the silliest thing I'd ever heard. "Let's get out," she said, unlocking the doors.

I locked my door back. "Are you out of your mind, heifer?"

"Then you stay out here." She got out of the car.

I hopped out and followed her like a fool. I was scared as we ran across the front yard. As soon as we got inside the house, a bunch of familiar faces popped out from everywhere shouting, "*Happy birthday!*"

I covered my face. "Oh my God!"

Cammy gave me a big hug. "I love you," she said.

I almost cried because I felt so bad after the way I'd treated her. I couldn't believe she'd planned all this for me. I got hugs from more folks than I could handle. Hollis tried to sneak and get one, but I wasn't with it. I let him know right away he'd better back up.

The DJ had his equipment set up in Cammy's mother's all-white dining room, and he had the place rocking to the Ying Yang Twins' "Salt Shaker." Cammy knew her mother would've had a fit if she found out people were tracking dirt in and out of her dining room. It seemed like Cammy invited every soul she knew. There were folks at my party that I'd never seen before in school. They were dancing, drinking, and smoking weed along the stairway. More people were still coming through the door too. All I could think was, *Cammy must've lost her mind.*

I made eye contact with Terrell, as he stood across the room drinking with his friends. They were looking at every girl that had on tight clothes. It seemed like all the hoochie mamas had to stop and smile in his face. I almost choked on my drink when he called me over. I crept away from my girls to see what he wanted. I swear it felt like I had to wait in line to get to him. As soon as his fan club disappeared, he handed me a gift bag. "Happy birthday. I hope you like it." He surprised me with a hug, sending electricity through my body.

"What is it?" I said.

"Open it and see." The smell of vodka was heavily on his breath.

I opened the bag, and inside was a lime-green thong bikini. I was speechless.

"I want you to wear it to Cancún, okay?"

I didn't know if he was kidding or not so I changed the subject. "How's your ankle?" I said, looking down to avoid eye contact.

"It's a'ight. Hopefully, it'll be ready to go next week. I gotta ball this year, but you didn't answer my question. Are you gonna wear it?"

"Andrea would have a fit."

"It's only a gift, and besides she's not even goin'," he said, taking a sip from his cup.

I got happy. "Maybe."

Everyone clung together like magnets when the DJ slowed the party down. "In Those Jeans" by Ginuwine had the room hot. I was tempted to grab Terrell until I saw him eyeing Shaneika in her skin-tight Baby Phat jeans. I was surprised she had his attention, considering her name had been run through the dirt on several occasions. She was a skank. Last year, she attended a party that Terrell's buddies threw for him, and got filthy drunk. A few of his boys ran a train on her and taped it. There were rumors that Terrell circulated the tape around school.

After all the embarrassment Shaneika had been through, she still thought she was the bomb because she was captain of the cheerleading team. I didn't know what had possessed Cammy to invite her to my party. After all the ass-kissing Cammy had done, it was a wonder she hadn't made the cheerleading team.

As the music played, Shaneika walked over and grabbed Terrell right from under my nose. I found a chair and flopped in it like I'd lost a heavyweight fight. I watched Terrell hold her tight in his arms, wishing it could be me. I was mad because it was my birthday and Shaneika was granted my wish. He laid his head on her shoulder. I could tell he was tipsy because his eyes were bloodshot red. I was glad he didn't have any car keys.

As they danced, I kept my eyes on Shaneika. She seemed to be enjoying the moment as she rubbed her hands all over Terrell's body. The tramp seized the moment while he was out of his right mind, knowing he had a girl. Suddenly, Shaneika got brave and kissed his lips. I wanted to get up and mop the floor with her raggedy weave. She started rolling her hips to the music. All the guys in the room were hypnotized. Terrell squeezed her butt cheeks like two melons, and started kissing her on the neck.

It was too much for me to handle.

Hollis walked over and invaded my space. His breath made me sick to the stomach. Mr. Drumline-Wannabe started bragging about his music scholarship to Grambling as if I actually cared. All I wanted him to do was disappear. I watched Shaneika guide Terrell out of the room. He could hardly stand up straight.

"Hollis, do me a favor," I said.

"What's that, sexy mango?"

"Go get me a soda out of the kitchen."

"Any particular kind?"

"No, just go." I almost died trying to hold my breath.

"Okay, I'll be right back."

Once he left, I exhaled. As Hollis headed towards the kitchen, I got up to spy on Shaneika and Terrell. They walked inside Cammy's mother's bedroom and locked the door. Cammy would've had a fit if she knew. I went to the bathroom entrance leading to the master bedroom. I prayed the door wouldn't be locked and it wasn't. When I cracked open the door, Terrell and Shaneika were tongue kissing on the bed. I knew the alcohol had him gone because he was not that type of guy.

Things got steamy when Shaneika took off her shirt. I almost lost it when Terrell started rubbing and sucking on her breasts. I was tempted to barge in on them, but that would've been lame. Out of all the guys at the party, Shaneika had to prey on the one that I completely adored.

As I stood at the door, more of their clothes hit the floor while they kissed. Terrell's body was fully aroused as his boxers descended.

I was so hurt when they started humping.

Suddenly, a devilish thought ran through my mind: Andrea would drop Terrell like a bad habit if she knew he was in bed with a girl. I couldn't wait to tell her everything.

Twenty minutes later, they stopped humping, and I ran away. But I kept my eyes on the bedroom from afar. After five minutes, Shaneika crept out the bedroom, looking around suspiciously. Several minutes later, I got up and walked into the bedroom. Terrell was lying on the bed butt naked, asleep. I threw a sheet over his waist, trying to avoid looking at his penis. It was apparent they had a blast because there was white stuff all over the sheets. Even though I was disgusted, I wanted to help Terrell get dressed before he got busted.

"Wake up, Terrell," I said, shaking him.

He opened his bloodshot eyes and smiled. "Come lay down."

"No."

"Why?"

"Because you're drunk."

"Am not," he slurred.

"Then get up before Cammy catches you in here."

He sat up and looked around, confused. "Where are my clothes?"

I handed him his shirt, boxers, and pants off the floor. Then he started getting dressed under the covers. "How was I?" he asked.

"Uh, Terrell, please snap out of it." I shook my head because I'd never seen him wasted before. After he got dressed, I helped him put on his shoes because he complained of dizziness, as he sat on the edge of the bed. Once I finished, I grabbed his strong arms and helped him up. He thanked me by throwing up on the carpet.

"No you didn't," I said, looking down at a pool of vomit. "We gotta clean you up."

"I'm sorry," he said, curling over.

I led him into the bathroom and gave him a full cap of Listerine. "Gargle it, Terrell. Your breath smells bad."

He swallowed the Listerine instead of gargling. "Damn, what you tryin' to do to me?"

I read the label. "You weren't supposed to swallow it, but you'll be okay." I grabbed a few towels and cleaned up his vomit off the bedroom floor. I never thought I'd be cleaning up after someone else's man. After I finished with the towels, I stuffed them in an empty Macy's bag to take out to the trashcan.

When I went back into the bathroom, Terrell was splashing cold water over his face. He looked at me through the mirror and said, "I'm gonna marry you one day. You're my angel."

"Sure, Terrell."

Suddenly, Eric stormed into the bathroom, breathless. "Yo, T, I've been looking all over the place for you. We gotta get you outta here!" he said, grabbing him.

Terrell stumbled and I caught him.

Eric looked at me. "What's his problem?"

"Too much to drink. Now what's your excuse?"

"I overheard Shaneika crying and telling a few people out there that T raped her."

My eyes almost popped out of my head. "For real?"

"Don't ask me any questions. Let's just bounce before she calls the police."

3

Two days after the party, Daddy told me that Terrell had been arrested for sexual assault. I couldn't believe the news until Eric confirmed it at the dinner table. Even then, I found it hard to believe that Terrell had been accused of rape. Reality struck me when I read Daddy's newspaper while sitting at the table. The story details were all wrong; the media had it twisted. I could recall every detail of that particular night; Shaneika gave it up like a free sample. And he wasn't the only one she'd let jump her bones. At 17 years old, Shaneika had a long track record, which I hoped came to the light.

After everyone left the kitchen, I sat at the table staring at Terrell's mug shot on the front page. The picture made him look like a thug. I was fuming.

The following day, school was "off glass." Terrell was the topic of everybody's conversation. Andrea was the first to jump to conclusions and judge him. She said if he'd given his life to the Lord, it would've never happened. I thought she was being cold-hearted. All through out that day, I had to put up with gossip and rumors. While everybody ran their traps, I knew the truth.

When I got home from school, I went straight to my bedroom. I didn't want to do anything even though I had a load of math homework. Instead of hitting the books, I laid in bed wondering what to do. It was a hard decision, but I'd made up my mind not to get involved considering Daddy's status. I thought it would've been unfair to ask him to get involved in the investigation when he'd been promoted less than five months ago. Besides that, people's eyes were already fixed on him because he was the first African-American Chief of Police in Dade County. *He'll probably face all kinds of scrutiny because I'm his daughter,* I thought. I refused to put my daddy through the headache.

As I lay in bed, I heard a knock at my bedroom door. When I opened the door, Daddy was standing there all smiles. He tried to put a smile on my face with a Michael Jackson dance.

"Daddy, I'm not feeling good," I said.

"Alright then I'll beat it, but not before you go take a look outside, baby girl."

I got excited, thinking Daddy had granted Terrell a get-out-of-jail-free card. "Who's outside?"

"It's a surprise."

I put on my shoes and rushed out the front door, hoping to see Terrell. When I didn't see him, I felt sad all over again. Ungrateful as it sounded, I'd rather it had been Terrell instead of a brand-new Honda Civic.

"Baby girl, put a smile on your face," Daddy said. Then he wrapped an arm around my shoulders and handed me the keys. "Won't you take your ol' man for a ride in your brand-new whip?"

"Thank you, Daddy," I smiled, hiding my true feelings. When I got inside the car, the new smell took my breath away.

Daddy plopped his long bones in the passenger's seat and opened the sunroof. The sunshine made his pecan-tan skin break out in a sweat. "I hope you don't have your little boyfriend in here," he said.

"I don't have a boyfriend, Daddy. That's the last thing on my mind," I lied.

Daddy raised his thick brows. "Then who was the young man I caught you talking to at one o'clock in the morning that night?"

"Oh, that was Terrell."

"You mean the knuckle-head football player who can't stay out of trouble?"

"Please don't judge him." I strapped on my seatbelt and took my new car for a spin.

While sitting in traffic, I broke the silence on Terrell. "Daddy, how much time could my friend get for rape?" I didn't want to bother Daddy about the situation but I couldn't help asking.

"It depends on the age of the victim, the circumstances of the alleged crime, and the criminal background of your friend."

"He's been arrested for drunk driving and driving with a suspended license." I hated revealing the list because I didn't want Daddy to look down on him.

"If convicted, he could be sentenced to the minimum of 10 years in prison."

"Oh my God!" I said, trembling. Then I started feeling guilty for not speaking up.

"Calm down. You need to wait until all the facts of the case come out. Rape is a serious offense. There may be evidence or witnesses that have yet to come forward." He shook his head. "These cats have to learn to use the head on their shoulders, instead of the one below their waists."

"He didn't do it, Daddy."

"I'm not questioning whether he did it or not. All I'm saying is these things can be avoided with discipline. I've been there plenty of times. But no means *no*."

⌘　⌘　⌘

After school, I went to the police department hoping I could get my hands on Terrell's incident report. I requested a copy of the report from the records division. The records clerk told me no because it was confidential information. I felt like cursing her out. Luckily, I saw Officer Jackson standing in the lobby reading a report. He was a good friend of the family; he and Daddy graduated from the police academy together. After saying hello, I begged him to get me a copy of the report. He locked his gun in his holster and then looked at me. I held my breath, hoping.

"Do you have a case number?" he said.

"No, but I have the person's name."

That should be good enough. I may also need a date of birth."

I gave him the information and waited in the lobby.

When he returned to the lobby, he gave me a five-minute speech. "I've had my fair share of run-ins with Internal Affairs. Keep your mouth zipped. If I get written up that's my behind."

I almost cried. "I won't tell a soul, Officer Jackson. Thank you so much."

I went outside and read the report while sitting in my car. I couldn't believe my eyes when I read, "Victim went to lie down in bedroom after feeling lightheaded when black male suspect walked in room and aggressively sought penetration . . ." After reading more, I was convinced that I had to stick up for Terrell. Everything I'd read in the report was a lie.

⌘　⌘　⌘

Days passed and I kept everything bottled up. Even though I knew Terrell was innocent, I wasn't confident that anyone would believe me. Besides, I was embarrassed for spying on them. I needed more time to think of the best way to proceed. I wanted to confide in Eric, but I was afraid he'd put too much pressure on Daddy and run him into the grave. Three years ago, Daddy had a mild stroke and scared all of us. I couldn't live with myself if I caused him another stroke.

In the wake of all the drama, I knew Terrell's grandmother, Miss Sheila, was having a fit. She'd been his guardian ever since he'd lost his mother to a heart attack, and his daddy had to be stationed overseas on active duty. Miss Sheila lived in the projects, but I never heard Terrell complain. He loved his grandmother to death. The lady was a faithful churchgoer and I hoped to God she was able to pray him out of this mess.

As I sat on the patio painting my toenails, Cammy called me talking trash. She actually believed that Terrell had done it. She made me sick with her ignorant comments. "He's gonna get his. I hope somebody breaks a broomstick off in his black ass," she said resentfully.

"That's wrong."

"No, what's *wrong* is him sticking his pita pecker in places it don't belong."

"You're only taking Shaneika's side because she's your girl."

"Right is right and wrong is wrong; he was wrong. Why are you defending him anyway? Every time somebody says something about him, it's Karla to the rescue —"

"I'm not defending anybody!"

"Don't be gettin' funky with me. These athletes always get off whenever they do something wrong instead of being punished like every other criminal. Hell, it's not fair."

"Do you really think Terrell would have to stoop that low to get some? We both know that Shanieka's loose."

"Who knows what could've happened when he got all horny?"

"You can say whatever you want to say, Cammy. Terrell didn't rape that girl."

"Whatever. He didn't have no business in my mama's bedroom to begin with. Some people don't have no kind of home training."

Look who's talking, I wanted to say. I hung up the phone before I ended up telling her off. I figured she was just suffering from pissed-at-men syndrome.

⌘　⌘　⌘

Three weeks later, Terrell was still locked up. Eric was emotional and it showed. At school he harassed people for information like he was a detective, and then at home he acted like a problem child. I'd never seen Eric act so mentally disturbed. He'd skip football practice, and on game nights he'd blow curfew. Two weeks ago, a FSU football recruiter came to the house, and Eric wouldn't come out of his room. He was taking Terrell's situation harder than me. I felt bad holding out on Eric but I didn't think he would believe me.

One evening, I knocked on Eric's bedroom door to check on him. He had Tupac's "Shed So Many Tears" on blast. I stood knocking at the door for a couple of minutes. Since he wouldn't open the door, I invited myself inside. The room was filled with smoke. My brother was sitting on the edge of his bed smoking weed. He was high. I put a hand on my hip. "Are you out of your mind, boy?" I said, fanning the air. I knew if Daddy came home, *it was on.*

Eric cut his eyes at me and kept puffing on the blunt.

I turned off the music and opened the windows to air out the room. Just then, Daddy pulled into the driveway in his unmarked police car.

"Eric, you need to put that mess out. Daddy's home," I warned him.

"I don't give a damn. What he gon' do to me?"

"You got issues."

I heard Daddy come in the front door. He came directly to Eric's room. "I know you aren't smoking marijuana in my house, boy!" he said.

Eric didn't say a word.

"Did you hear me?" Daddy yelled.

Eric cut his eyes at Daddy, looking strung out. "What you gon' do? Take me to jail, Chief?"

Daddy raised his eyebrows. "What did you just say to me, boy?"

"Did I stutter?"

Daddy walked over to the bed and dared Eric to repeat himself.

Eric stood up. "Did I stutter, punk?" he repeated boldly.

Daddy shoved Eric. Suddenly, all hell broke loose. They began throwing powerful punches at each other. I didn't know what to do. I'd never seen them go at each other before. They turned the room upside down as I pleaded for them to stop. My mother had picked a fine time to get home late. Lately it seemed as though she was more concerned with the kids at her school than her own children. But if she didn't get home quick, she was going to be minus a child. When I saw blood, I was tempted to call 911. Eric's mouth was bleeding on the carpet.

All of a sudden, Daddy fell on his knees, clutching his chest.

I ran to his side while he hyperventilated. *"What did you do?"* I screamed at Eric.

"Nothin' shoot," he said stubbornly.

"Why do you have to act like a thug all the time? Go call emergency!"

Eric stood there breathing hard. "What's the number?"

The weed had him gone. "You can't be for real. It's 911," I said, shaking my head.

"9-1-1," he kept repeating to himself as if the number was hard to remember. He ran out of the room while I stayed at Daddy's side.

Daddy moaned in pain.

Five minutes later, the ambulance pulled up in the yard. As soon as the paramedics rushed through the room, Daddy acted like everything was all right. He hated hospitals.

The paramedics checked his blood pressure and it was high.

Mommy came running in the bedroom. She looked at Daddy down on the floor and shouted, "Oh Jesus!"

"Mommy, calm down; he's fine," I said.

She put a hand over her chest and took a deep sigh. "What happened?"

"I'll let Eric tell you," I said.

Mommy went to the hospital with Daddy. I wanted to slap Eric into the middle of next week while he stood in the hallway rolling another blunt. The incident with Daddy would've never happened if it weren't for him acting stupid. Eric was lucky Daddy didn't die, because I would've ate him alive.

⌘　⌘　⌘

The next morning, I was glad to see Daddy in the kitchen. He was moving around as if nothing happened. The doctors had given him a shot for muscle spasms and then released him.

After Daddy made a bowl of oatmeal, he sat at the table. I felt on edge while I watched him eat. I wanted to tell him about Terrell, but then I didn't. There was too much tension in the house and the last thing I wanted to do was aggravate him. The whole situation was beginning to take a toll on me. From what I'd read in the paper, it seemed like Terrell was going down. My conscience was killing me. Not only could Terrell serve serious time if found guilty, but now none of the Division-One schools that'd been scouting him were interested anymore. This was supposed to be his breakout season, but instead he was looking at time. I couldn't picture Terrell spending 10 years in prison with a bunch of thugs and killers. I'd heard messed-up stories about what goes on in prison, like men turning each other out. The thought of Terrell getting turned out made me sick to the stomach.

⌘　⌘　⌘

A week later, I caught Daddy relaxing in the den. He had his feet propped on the coffee table watching the news. I wished he focused his mind on other things instead of police work. I gave Daddy a hug, thinking to myself I could've lost him. After I checked how he was feeling, I made my way into the kitchen. Eric was bussin' suds. I sat down at the table with a lot on my mind.

Seconds later, Daddy walked in the kitchen and washed out a glass. I was surprised he and Eric were breathing the same air. I had my fingers crossed, hoping they didn't cross paths. Daddy fixed a glass of orange juice and then slammed the refrigerator. After he walked out of the kitchen, Eric shook his head. "That fool is trippin'," he said.

"You owe him an apology," I said.

"No, I owe him a beat down."

"You get on my nerves."

Eric tossed a dishtowel into the sink and then sat at the table. Suddenly, a good idea popped into my head. I thought of calling Miss Sheila and telling her everything. I was willing to take the stand and testify if need be. I would've done anything as long as it didn't involve Daddy.

I grabbed the portable phone off the counter. "What's Miss Sheila's number?" I said, sitting back down.

"For what?"

"I need to talk to her."

"No way. His grandma isn't in a good state of mind right now."

"I need to tell her something."

"Tell her what?"

"Terrell didn't rape Shaneika."

Eric stared at me like I was stupid. "No, duh. Don't you think everybody already knows that, dummy?"

I stayed calm instead of going off on him. "Cammy seems to think otherwise."

"That girl's got mental problems. She's the only one who thinks he's guilty. My homie don't have to steal no coochie. Everybody knows Shaneika is making this up to get back at him for spreading that flick around school."

I set the phone down. "I give up."

Eric leaned up in his chair, eyeing me. "What makes you think calling his grandma is gonna do any good?"

Finally, I felt it was time to open up. I was tired of bearing the guilt. "Because I saw the whole thing, Sherlock."

"What'd you mean you saw the whole thing?"

"Just take my word."

He hopped up and stood over me like he was upset. "You big dummy! Why didn't you speak up?"

I snapped. "I don't know who the hell you think you're talking to!"

He calmed down. "I'm sorry."

"You better recognize," I said, rolling my eyes.

He sat down. "You better learn to open your mouth and speak up. A black man's life is at stake right now."

"I didn't think y'all would believe me."

"You need to mention this to your daddy."

"No, I'm not mentioning anything to him. He's under enough stress as it is."

"My dawg's life is depending on this, and all you can think about is that chump being stressed? Stress is when you have to worry about your salad being tossed."

I crossed my arms stubbornly. "I said I'll talk to Miss Sheila and that's it."

He bit down on his bottom lip. "Oooh, I could strangle you. There's already enough brothers serving time in the pen for crimes they didn't commit."

"Then you tell him." I was certain he wouldn't do it.

"I don't have nothing to say to him."

"Terrell needs our help. So what are you going to do?"

He picked up the phone and called Miss Sheila. Unfortunately, she didn't pick up.

"Man, we're gonna have to keep calling. Hopefully, she'll pick up sooner or later," he said.

Mommy walked in the kitchen while we were talking. She had a hairnet wrapped over her pretty black curls, and her bronze-colored skin was glowing. She sliced a grapefruit and then sat at the table. "What are you two in here plotting?" she said, eyeing us.

"Nothing," I said.

"We're trying to get my homie out of jail. We need you to talk to Uncle Tom."

"Alright, boy, watch your mouth," Mommy said, eating her grapefruit. "You two don't go bothering with your daddy. Case closed."

Eric shook his head.

"I want both of you to come to church with me tomorrow," she said.

Eric looked at Mommy like she had bumped her head. "I'm not going to Andrea's daddy's boring church. He preaches too long and there don't ever be no fine girls. Last time I went to that church it was *Thriller* Sunday."

Mommy started laughing.

"That jive ain't funny, Ma; like New Edition, you got to count me out."

"I'll go," I said.

"Good for you," she said. After finishing her grapefruit, she got up and turned in for bed.

I got up next. "Eric, you should come with us."

"Ugh, no thank you. No girls, no me."

"Is that all you think about? There's more to life than girls. Do it for Terrell, gosh. You know his grandmother never misses a service."

He sighed. "Let me think about it and I'll get back with you."

"Forget it," I said, walking out of the kitchen.

⌘ ⌘ ⌘

I laid across my bed and called Cammy. I begged her to come to church with me because I didn't want to handle the pressure alone. It was too bad she couldn't go; her folks wouldn't let her out the house except for school. She was in big trouble. The so-called rape incident that happened at Cammy's house may've jeopardized her mother's chances for re-election. The media had a field day making her mom look bad. To add insult to injury, Cammy's folks had $15,000 worth of jewelry stolen on the night of the party. I felt bad as Cammy gave me the scoop. I was speechless. Even though Cammy couldn't go, I didn't let it discourage me. I'd held back long enough and I was ready to speak up.

⌘ ⌘ ⌘

The next morning when I opened my eyes, Eric was standing over me. He was dressed in a nice beige suit. "Wake up, Whoopi!" he said, smashing my head into the pillow.

"I'm up."

"Hurry up, sinner, we're waiting on you."

"If you get out!" After he left, I got ready for church.

When we got to church, it was a full house. Eric's eyes lit up upon seeing all the pretty girls in the building. "Damn!" he said, walking through the door.

Mommy popped him across the head with her church program. "Cut it out."

"My bad," he said, fixing his tie.

We found seats in the balcony. I spotted Andrea sitting in the choir stand dressed in all white. She looked like a sad angel. She'd been taking things hard. She spotted me and smiled. I hadn't seen her smile in weeks.

The choir stood up to sing. Andrea grabbed the mic and led solo. Her voice sounded like a beautiful melody sent from heaven.

"Sang, girl!" the fat lady behind us shouted, waving her flabby arms.

I smiled and started clapping to the hymn. As Andrea sang, I browsed the room looking for Miss Sheila. I was disappointed when I didn't see her. If I had known she wasn't coming I wouldn't have come. Eric was right: Andrea's daddy's sermons were long and boring. To top that, he took up too many offerings.

After the choir finished, Andrea's daddy got up and began his sermon, titled: "All Things Are Possible If We Believe." For once, I didn't fall asleep in church, because the message was good.

After service ended, Andrea ran up and hugged me. "Oh my goodness, I can't believe you came!" she said. "Did I sound okay?"

I smiled. "Ashanti doesn't have anything on you, girl."

"Thank you. I've been working hard."

"It's paid off because you sounded good."

Eric walked across our path engaged in conversation with a chocolate cutie pie.

"Oh, Lord," Andrea said, rolling her eyes at him. "I hope he doesn't mess over Lisa."

"Don't worry yourself, he will," I said, shaking my head. "Have you talked to Terrell lately?"

"He called collect last night." She sounded hurt.

"How are things looking for him?"

She took a deep breath. "We'll have to wait and see what happens. It's not in our hands."

Contrary to her belief, I felt Terrell's freedom was in my hands.

4

An entire month passed and we hadn't heard from Miss Sheila. I'd been to her apartment on several occasions hoping she'd answer. I refused to give up. No one had heard a word from Terrell either. One day I went to the jail to see him, but he refused visitation. Sometimes I cried myself to sleep thinking about him.

As I sat in my room staring at the walls, I decided to do the unthinkable. I stepped to Daddy while he was outside vacuuming his car. I waited patiently as he finished. When he turned off the vacuum, I cleared my throat loudly. "Daddy, I need to talk to you for a minute," I said.

"What's up, baby girl?" He started cleaning the windows with Windex, not giving me his full attention.

I was getting impatient with him. "Daddy, can you stop for a minute?"

He stopped and looked at me. "Before we start, answer this: am I gonna have to shoot somebody's son?"

I smiled. "No."

He looked relieved. "Oh, okay."

Daddy listened to me as I told him what happened at the party. I felt uncomfortable while I gave him the details. It was the first time I'd ever talked to him about things pertaining to sex. "He had a bit too much to drink," I said, "but he didn't force himself on her; she gave it up."

"Is that right?"

"I swear it, Daddy."

"I wish there was something I could do, baby."

"What do you mean? You're the chief."

"You have to let the judicial system do its part."

"What about your part?"

He didn't say anything but I could read his mind.

"I'm telling you the truth," I pleaded.

"Look, I know you don't want to see your little boyfriend do any time in prison, but this isn't the way to go about it —"

"Forget I said anything." I knew he didn't believe me, which was the reason I didn't want to tell him in the first place. All the same, I was really hurt. I was walking towards the front door when he called me. "Yes?" I said, feeling let down.

"I don't want to hear anything else about you riding through Liberty City. Don't think I don't have my ear to the streets at all times."

"I don't believe I'm better than my own people." I couldn't believe I'd said that to Daddy.

His shoulders swelled. "And I'm glad you think that way, but the truth is your own people can be your worst enemy. You'll see one day."

I didn't pay Daddy any mind because he was acting uppity.

After I went back inside the house, I locked myself in my bedroom and started reading *Coffee Will Make You Black* by April Sinclair. I felt down in the dumps. I thought it was a crying shame that Daddy refused to honor justice. Truthfully, I didn't think he wanted to put his name on the line for Terrell. If push came to shove, I was willing to go to the state attorney's office. I only wished I had someone in my corner before I took matters into my own hands.

Someone knocked at my door. "Who is it?" I said.

"Me."

I got up and unlocked the door for Eric. "What?" I said.

"What did he say?"

"He doesn't believe me."

"Damn, that's messed up," he sighed.

"We just can't give up."

⌘　⌘　⌘

The next day after school, I found myself at Miss Sheila's door again. I was nervous, as usual. I knocked on the door and a man answered; he looked in his mid-forties. He was dark, handsome, and clean-shaven. I was at a loss for words because I didn't expect to see a tall good-looking man standing over me.

"Terrell isn't home right now," he said, preparing to close the door.

"Yes, sir, I know . . . but I'm here to see Miss Sheila."

"She's in the kitchen," he said, letting me in.

"Thank you." I stepped into the apartment. Terrell's grandmother had his pictures and trophies in a glass showcase. She seemed proud of him. As my eyes wandered, I noticed the apartment was worn down. The carpet looked old and dirty, and the walls were screaming for a fresh coat of paint. I couldn't imagine living in the small cluttered box. Now I could understand why Terrell always talked about going pro; he wanted to move his grandmother out the slums.

"Are you Terrell's girlfriend?" the man asked.

I blushed. "No, we're good friends."

He shook my hand. "I'm Terrell's father, Kenny."

I was deeply honored. "It's nice to meet you, Mr. Lewis. I'm Karla."

"Please, call me Kenny," he said. His smile made me feel comfortable.

"Okay, Kenny it is." I didn't know Terrell's father was back in town, but it felt good to know that Miss Sheila wasn't in this thing alone.

Kenny led me into the kitchen. Miss Sheila was sitting at the table eating boiled peanuts. The chipped cabinets, rotted countertops, and gooey rattraps caught my eye. The roaches were running wild, but I acted like I didn't see them.

"This beautiful young lady is here to see you," Kenny said, setting his hand on my shoulder.

She squinted. "Is that Andrea?"

"No, ma'am; I'm Karla."

"I don't think we've met." Miss Sheila made me feel unimportant, not remembering me from church. But I was glad to see that her smooth jet-black skin hadn't aged. "Who are your peoples?"

"Norris Johnson is my father."

"Yeah, I know the Johnsons; they're good peoples," she said, smiling. Miss Sheila offered me a seat at the table and then asked, "What made the wind blow your hips through my door?"

Kenny excused himself from the room as we talked. I couldn't believe I was sitting face-to-face with the most important woman in Terrell's life. I felt bad when she told me she'd been in and out of the hospital battling high blood pressure. If I had known she was sick, I wouldn't have popped up to her home unexpectedly. During our conversation, she told me that Kenny had taken an emergency leave because of all the drama going on. Usually, Terrell was the one who looked after his grandmother, but with him being locked away, it left everyone in a bad position. Deep into our conversation, I felt nervous as I explained to Miss Sheila what happened at the party. I let her know I was willing to do whatever it took to help Terrell, even if it meant taking the witness stand. As I finished telling my story, she began crying tears of joy. Then she hugged me tightly; I thought I was going to pop.

"Lord, knows I've done my best to raise my grandson the right way. I knew he didn't do such a thing. I can't wait to tell Kenny!" she said.

At that moment, I felt like a heroine as I watched Miss Sheila dance around the kitchen, slinging her jheri curl. I thought her frail body was going to fall apart.

"Sugar, if you ever need anything you better call me. You hear me?" she said.

"Yes, ma'am."

⌘ ⌘ ⌘

The next day, I went to the jail with Miss Sheila and Kenny. It felt awkward going to see Terrell in jail instead of on the football field. Goose bumps had risen on my skin, as Kenny and I sat inside the visitor's room, waiting to see him first. Finally, he walked in the room wearing an orange uniform. His hair was thick and he looked angry. He sat and picked up the phone. "Man, what you brought her here for!" he yelled through the phone.

I was offended as I read his lips. "I'll leave," I said, turning to Kenny.

"Don't leave," he said, placing a hand on my shoulder. "Boy, shut up and listen! She's here because she wants to help you!"

"There ain't nothin' she can do for me, goddamnit. Matter of fact, why don't y'all both haul ass?"

I couldn't believe Terrell.

"Listen to me; you gotta let somebody help you, son," Kenny said.

"I'm a black man. Ain't nothin' she can do for me!"

"Son, listen to me . . ."

Terrell hung up the phone and folded his arms stubbornly.

"Pick up the phone, boy!" Kenny said.

Terrell ignored his father.

Kenny got up. "I give up. I'll let his grandmother deal with him," he said, walking out of the room.

After Kenny left, Terrell glared at me with a cold look. For some reason, it was hard to look him in the eye, but I managed to do it. A minute later, Miss Sheila entered the visitor's room. Terrell picked up the phone without hesitation.

"Hey, baby," Miss Sheila said, putting the phone to her ear.

Terrell looked at her sadly. I read his lips when he said, "What is she doing here?"

"The grace of God led her this way —"

Terrell slammed the phone on the hook and walked out of the room. Miss Sheila shook her head and looked at me. She had tears in her eyes. "Please don't give up on my grandson like he's already given up on himself."

I hugged Miss Sheila. "Everything's going to be okay," I said, tearing up.

After our trip to the jail, we visited the state attorney's office where I presented my story.

5

Two weeks later, I decided to let go and let God. I figured the truth would come out during Terrell's hearing in two months.

One evening, I flipped the TV to *Jenny Jones*. They were discussing cheating boyfriends. Things started heating up and I was deep into it. As I screamed at the dumb girls on TV, someone rang the doorbell. I sucked my teeth. "Please go away," I mumbled under my breath.

The doorbell kept singing. A commercial came on and I ran to get the door. I squinted through the peephole. I almost died when I saw Terrell standing there in the flesh. "Hold on," I said, running to the bathroom. I had to make sure I was perfect. I had on a cute denim dress, which I unbuttoned to let my lace bra show. Then I raced back to the front door.

When I opened the door, Terrell looked nervous. He had on a tank top and a pair of khaki-colored cargo shorts. I watched his eyes penetrate my top.

"Is Eric home?" he said.

I looked down and pretended to be surprised that my boobies were out. "Oh excuse me," I said, buttoning up my dress. "No, he isn't home."

"Tell him I stopped by." Terrell walked away but then stopped and came back. "Before I go, I wanna say that I appreciate what you did for me. Thanks to you all the charges were dropped. It takes heart to stand up for somethin' that's right. I almost wanna squeeze you in my arms." He smiled and shook his head like it was a close call. "Instead, I'll say thank you."

My heart felt like it had jumped into my throat. "You're welcome."

"Don't forget to tell Eric that I dropped by." He turned and walked away.

I wanted to invite him inside but I couldn't fix my lips to ask. After I closed the door, I watched him through the window. He got in the car with his friends. All of sudden, he got back out of the car, and rang the doorbell again.

I opened the door. "Yes?"

"What you doin' tomorrow night?" he asked me.

I played it cool. "I dunno, why?"

"We should catch a movie or somethin'?"

I let the surprise show on my face. "What about Andrea?"

He shrugged his shoulders and looked at me. "It's only a movie; we ain't hurtin' nobody."

I shrugged too. "Sounds good to me."

"We'll catch a nine o'clock show."

Are you crazy? I thought. I knew my parents wouldn't let me out of the house that late on a school night. My folks didn't play that mess. "Why so late?" I said.

"I have football practice." His forehead crinkled like he was worried. "Is that gonna be a problem?"

"Pla-eeze, I'm a big girl."

"I see." He grinned, looking at my body. "I'm gon' need you to pick me up. Is that a'ight?"

I could care less about him not having a car. "Not a problem," I said.

After he left for good, I ran straight to my closet, screaming at the top of my lungs. It was a good thing that no one was home, because I couldn't control myself. I searched through my clothes for the perfect outfit. Everything I had was too conservative. For my first date, I wanted to show off my body. I was seventeen years old for crying out loud! I decided to leap over the edge: I called Cammy and asked if I could borrow something out of her closet. Of course she had to be nosy and ask me who was the lucky guy taking me out. I lied and told her Rashard, hoping it wouldn't backfire. I felt like a hypocrite, but I didn't dare tell her the truth. She probably would've thought I was a snake. But the truth of the matter was, I liked Terrell before Andrea.

⌘　⌘　⌘

The next night, I lied to my parents in order to get out of the house. I told them I had a group project to do. I knew they wouldn't have let me out on a date with Terrell. My daddy would've had him fingerprinted and all. Mommy worse, though. I figured it was because she got pregnant at an early age.

I searched through Cammy's closet for an outfit. Most of her things were too sleazy for me. I wasn't used to wearing clothes with my boobies and back out; I would've felt like a hoochie. I decided to keep what I had on, which was a sweater and a long skirt. There was no way I was walking out the door looking like a hooker.

Cammy got mad. "I can't believe you're gonna wear that mess," she said, turning up her lip.

"It's better than wearing nothing at all. Shoot, it's cold outside."

"Stop making excuses. You're too old fashioned for your own good. Rashard needs to see that cute shape so he can spend some bread." Cammy handed me an outfit and shoved me in the bathroom. "Please change before you embarrass yourself. I'd hate for you to go out like that on your first date." She handed me a pair of pink stilettos too.

"These are too high," I said, looking at the five-inch heel.

"Girl, stop tripping," she said, closing the bathroom door.

Just to shut her up, I changed into the Fuchsia halter top and tight mini. The outfit was cute, but I felt naked as I stared in the mirror.

I walked out of the bathroom and Cammy looked me over.

"Now that's what I'm talking about," she smiled. "Go get him, girl!"

As I walked out of Cammy's bedroom, I paused. "Wait," I said.

"What's wrong?"

"I need to call Eric and tell him not to put on the alarm."

"Girl, go, I'll tell him," she said, grabbing her cell phone off the dresser.

When I walked outside, it was freezing. I couldn't believe I'd let Cammy talk me into wearing a hoochie mama outfit. As I got in the car, I reminded her to cover for me if my folks called looking for me.

"I got you, boo," she winked.

When I got to Terrell's place, I was scared to get out. I didn't want to get mugged and I didn't want Miss Sheila to see me dressed like a hoochie. Fortunately, Terrell came outside right on time. He jogged to the car and got in, looking shocked. I felt overdressed, while he looked comfortable in a pair of jeans and a Randy Moss jersey. "Dang, girl, you look good," he said. "Like P: 'Make 'em say ugh!'"

I laughed.

As I focused my attention on the road, I felt Terrell staring at me. One time I turned and caught him looking at my thighs. I felt like the biblical whore, Jezebel. I turned on the music to distract his attention away from me. He started bobbing his head to "Butterflies" by Alicia Keys.

"That's one talented chick," he said. Then he turned down the radio and focused his attention on me again. "Why do I sense that you nervous?"

I shrugged. "Maybe I should take you back home," I said, looking out the rearview mirror at the car trailing us. I was paranoid. It would've been my luck that it was Andrea. I took a deep breath when they turned off at the next intersection.

"Why?" he said.

"It should be obvious. I mean, what if we bump into somebody?"

"I don't care what anybody thinks of us. You were there for me — I only wish I could pay you back."

I wanted to scream, but I played it cool. "Terrell, you don't owe me anything."

"I don't think you understand the capacity of what you did. If it weren't for you, I'd be just another number in the system. I tell you one thing, Ion't never wanna get wasted like that anymore. I was so drunk that I don't even remember sleepin' wit' that girl."

"I only did the right thing," I said. I tried not to relive the scene of him lying across the bed naked, but I couldn't help it because he was blessed in the right place.

"And I can't thank you enough, girl. One thing I've learned is that when the going gets tough, you can count all your friends on one hand . . ." The glare in his eyes gave me insight to his broken heart. "I feel like Andrea let me down at a time in my life when I needed her the most."

"You know she means well."

"She's so wrapped in her Bible that she's gonna end up losing a *good thing*. I mean, she won't even let me touch her. You'd think after all this time we'd be crushin'."

I felt like he was getting a bit too personal.

"I could cheat but I ain't that type of dude."

"Maybe she's saving herself for marriage."

"I respect that but I've been waiting for a long time. The sex is due to me. I'm not some cat she just met yesterday, you know. I got needs."

"I hear you."

I pulled into the movie theatre parking lot. We sat in the car while he continued to vent. "I've compromised in this relationship, so why can't she? I go to church, I read my Bible, and I've even fasted. Do you know I've even given up eating pork? She has me making sacrifices, yet she's not willing to meet me half way." He stared at me while opening his door. "I hate to say it but I'm ready to move on, Karla."

As we sat in the movie theatre watching *Dreamgirls,* time began ticking away in my mind. I knew my mother had called Cammy's house because it was going on twelve o'clock. I looked at Terrell and he seemed to be enjoying the movie. I tried to build up the nerve to tell him that I needed to get home, but I couldn't. The last thing I wanted him to do was laugh at me. Terrell moved closer to me and I began to feel uncomfortable. All I could think about was Andrea, and what if she knew that Terrell had placed his arm around my shoulders. Terrell looked me in the eye as if he knew I couldn't resist his charm. Then he smiled at me, as if he knew how weak I was when it came to the scent of his cologne and his gorgeous smile.

I forced my attention back to the big screen, refusing to fall into his trap.

After the movie, I didn't waste any time getting out the door. I almost broke my neck, tripping in Cammy's stilettos.

"Whoa, slow down before you hurt yourself," Terrell said, catching me.

So much for hoping he didn't see me trip. I was so embarrassed that I wanted to scream.

"Why are you in such a rush?" he asked, trying to keep up. "Slow down."

I took his advice before I embarrassed myself again. The cold had me shivering. Goose bumps had spread over my arms and legs. Terrell must have felt sorry for me because he wrapped me in his arms from behind. I got nervous when I felt him breathing down my neck.

"Is that better?" he whispered softly in my ear.

"Yes." I felt like the luckiest girl on earth.

"It's my pleasure, beautiful."

When we got in the car, I was a little sad because I didn't want the night to end. Still, I sped to Terrell's crib, worried about how late it was. I pulled into a parking space so fast that I almost rode over the stomp.

"What you tryin' to do, kill me?" he said. "Next time we go out, I'm driving." He was quiet for a moment, then he looked at me. "Will there be a next time?"

I looked down. "I hope so."

"I hope so too." He got out of the car and then walked over to my side. "Open the door," he said, pulling on the handle.

"No way, it's too cold."

"Karla, open the door." He started bouncing like he was trying to keep warm.

I opened the door and got out. I figured if I was going to get grounded, I might as well make it worth while. Terrell reached out his arms for me. I leaped over my guilty conscience and landed into his strong arms. He hugged me so tight that if I had silicone breasts, they would've leaked. "I don't know what I would've done without you," he said, pressing his face against my neck. "For the first time in my life, I was afraid."

I told him that I couldn't breathe, and he eased up.

"I'm sorry," he said, leaning on the car. Then he gently pulled me close. "Put your arms around me. Don't be scared."

Feeling timid, I placed my arms around him. I felt uncomfortable pressed against the bulge in his pants. "I think I should go," I said.

"Won't you come inside for a minute?"

I imagined going inside and Terrell making sweet love to me. My mind was in LaLa land, as I envisioned his lips and body pressed against mine. Then I pictured his tongue climbing down my spine . . .

"Is that a yes or no?" he said, rubbing my back.

I snapped back to reality. "Huh?"

"I said do you wanna come in?"

"No, I can't; I have to get home," I said firmly.

"That's understandable. I don't mean to be so greedy, but I know we may never get this opportunity again. I can picture your brother killin' me."

"I think Andrea would kill you first."

"I'm not sweatin' it. The truth of the matter is she didn't keep it 100 while I was locked up. Her and her family looked down on me instead of lifting a brother up," he nodded.

He stared me in the eye and I looked away. I was battling pure guilt.

"Why can't you look me in the eye?" he said.

I shrugged.

"Look at me, Karla." He gently touched my face.

I looked him in the eye.

"See, was that so hard? I want you to call me when you get home."

"Okay."

"You sure you don't wanna come in?"

"I'm positive."

"Can I give you a kiss?" he said, still looking into my eyes.

I didn't know what to say, so I stood there speechless.

Terrell took the initiative and softly pressed his lips against mine. We kissed for five seconds. "I'm gonna let you get home," he said.

I was shocked that we had kissed.

"Are you okay?" he said.

"Yes, I'm . . . fine," I stuttered.

He laughed. "Thanks for kickin' it wit' me tonight."

"You're welcome." I got in the car and cranked up.

"Don't forget to call me," he said, running to the front door.

When I left, I thought about Terrell all the way home without a single interruption.

⌘　⌘　⌘

I pulled into my parents' driveway at 1:45 AM. I went through the backyard to sneak into the house. I stepped in dog crap. I almost vomited when I felt it mush between my toes. I wanted to kill my next-door neighbors' mutt. Cammy would've had a fit if she knew what her shoes had been through. As soon as I touched my bedroom window, the alarm went off. My heart jumped out of my chest. Hurdling over bushes and sprinklers, I ran back to the front of the house before Daddy came outside with his pistol. He'd shoot anything that moved. My daddy looked out the window.

I waved to let him know that it was me.

Eric opened the door and laughed. "Busted!" he said.

I wanted to strangle his no-good ass.

"Go to bed, Eric," Daddy said.

Eric left the room laughing. "That's what you get."

I wanted to crawl underneath a rock when I realized that I was still in Cammy's clothes.

Mommy looked me over as if she wanted to strangle me. "Where've you been dressed like a whore?" she said.

"Woman, don't talk to my daughter that way," Daddy butted in.

Mommy put a hand on her hip, cutting him down to size. "When your daughter ends up pregnant, I'm going to let you deal with it!" She pointed in his face, then she stormed into their bedroom and slammed the door.

I looked at my poor daddy. "I'm sorry," I said.

"That's okay. Just go get me a blanket, baby girl."

I got a blanket off my bed and gave it to Daddy. He stretched out on the couch and looked at me. "As long as you live, don't you ever walk in this house at two o' clock in the morning. You hear me?"

"Uh huh," I said.

"I'm not playing with you. Don't let it happen again. It's fools out there . . ."

Nights like this made me wish I were away in college. After Daddy finished his lecture, I went in my bedroom and called Terrell. I'd planned to make it quick, so I could scrub myself clean in the shower.

"What's up?" he answered.

"I made it home."

"Darn, you must've flew." Silence took over the phone for a few seconds. "I'm freezing," he said, breaking the silence. "I wish I had you here to keep me warm."

I was wishing the same thing. As I sat on the phone with him, the smell of dog crap became unbearable. "Terrell, I gotta go take a shower," I said.

"Okay, I'll talk to you later. Think about me, okay?"

"Yes, Terrell, and goodnight," I smiled.

⌘   ⌘   ⌘

During English class, I felt bad looking into Andrea's eyes knowing I had been out with her boyfriend. I'd heard of other girls fooling around with their best friend's man, but I never thought I'd be a suspect. I made a promise I'd never do it again.

After school, Cammy and Andrea followed me to my car. We noticed a rose sitting on my windshield. Andrea picked it up. "Look at what we have here," she said, taking a whiff. "Someone thinks you're special."

"I wonder who," I said, suspecting Terrell.

Cammy pointed out the card on the ground. She reached down to pick it up, but I shoved her out of the way. "Move, I got it!" I said.

Cammy put a hand over her chest as if her feelings were hurt. "Excuse me."

"What is wrong with you, child?" Andrea said.

"Nothing."

"We're not letting you leave until you read the card," Cammy said.

"Yes, read the card," Andrea said.

"Right now?"

Cammy rolled her eyes to the sky. "Nah, tomorrow, heffa."

I slowly unsealed the edges of the envelope. My heart was pounding as they glared over my shoulder. Eric snuck up behind Cammy and snatched her away. During the commotion, I slid the card inside my book bag while nobody was looking.

Andrea looked at her watch. "I wish Terrell would come on before he makes me late for choir rehearsal."

A second later, Terrell pulled up in Andrea's Volkswagen Beetle. Andrea told me bye and then got in the car with him. As she put on her seatbelt, Terrell winked at me. I smiled and waved goodbye to them. Then I got in my car, thanking the man upstairs for delivering me from Andrea's wrath. I opened the card and it only read "Thinking of You" with a smiley face. Terrell hadn't signed it. He must've known Andrea would be around when I got it.

⌘　⌘　⌘

That evening, I was in a singles chat room when Daddy told me that I had company. I peeked in the den, spotting Terrell. I couldn't believe he'd had popped up. He must've had lost his mind. I went in the den. He and Daddy were talking football.

"Have you decided who you're going to sign with?" Daddy said.

"No, not yet." Terrell seemed comfortable talking to Daddy.

"You know, the Hurricanes could use a deep threat like yourself."

Terrell smiled. "I take it you like the 'Canes?"

"I'm a Hurricane for life," Daddy said, chuckling. "We'd certainly like to have you. You almost put me in mind of Santana Moss, except you have more size than him. I think you'd fit well into U.M.'s program."

"I bet," Terrell smiled.

I had to drag Terrell out of the room before Daddy bribed him to death. "What are you doing here?" I said, whispering in the hallway. "Eric isn't home."

"I came to see you. I had a good time last night."

I blushed. "Thank you. I had a nice time, too."

He flashed a cute grin. "Hopefully, you'll let me take you out this weekend?"

I pretended to be offended. "What kind of friend would I be if I were to keep going out with you?"

"If I'm happy and you're happy then I don't see what's the problem." Terrell followed me into my bedroom. "Use Your Heart" by SWV was playing on HOT 105. Terrell shook his head while looking around at the posters on my wall. "I see you're a true-live Usher fan. That cat got all the females caught up." He sat at the computer desk and asked if he could check his email.

"Go ahead," I said.

He started reading his messages. I peeped over his shoulder and saw a half-naked picture of Andrea. She was lying across her bed in her bra and panties. *Not Ms. Holy!* I giggled.

Terrell looked at me. "What's so funny?"

"Oh, nothing."

He closed his Hotmail and then focused his attention on me. "Did I surprise you wit' the rose?"

I shoved him. "Yes, you did — and don't be doing that crap."

He raised his eyebrows. "A cat like me goes out of my way to buy you a card and a rose, and this is the thanks I get?"

"Under the circumstances you know what I meant, boy."

Terrell started moving his neck from side to side like he was in pain.

"What's wrong?" I said.

"My shoulders are tight from lifting. I hate lifting weights."

"Is there something I can do?" I wanted to slap myself for sounding so eager.

"Yeah, come here, gal," he said, grabbing my hips. "I need a real good massage." Terrell placed my hands on his strong shoulders. As I started rubbing his shoulders, I had to blink a few times. It seemed like I'd dreamed this a million times. Terrell and I started talking about things: prom, the senior class trip to Cancún, graduation, college. I think I was the only one that knew he'd planned on signing with USC, because he made me promise not to tell a soul. While the media and major universities were busy speculating about his future, I knew the answer. I felt special being the person to hold Terrell's secrets.

As we were talking, someone tapped on the door. When I heard a bunch of giggling, I knew it was Cammy and Andrea. Terrell hopped up like a jack-in-the-box and so did I. He scrambled around the room trying to find a place to hide. I shoved him in the closet, and he almost fell tripping over my shoes.

When I opened the door, Andrea asked me if I'd seen him.

"No," I said.

"That's funny; my car is outside."

"Him and Eric went to the park," I lied.

"Are you serious? That heathen was supposed to pick me up from choir rehearsal. Next time his broke behind needs to use my car, he'll be catching the metro rail. I can't believe he would do this to me."

"Oh, get over it," Cammy said. "Anyway, chile, I just came to get my top, but the shitty shoes you can keep, boo-boo. Don't ever say I've never given you nothing."

"I disinfected the shoes with bleach, Cammy. Gosh."

"And what is your point?" Cammy walked over to the closet. When she opened the closet, she froze and then looked at me, closing it shut. "We need to go," she said.

Andrea got up from the computer desk. "If you see Terrell tell him that I said his behind is mine."

Cammy looked at me with a question mark on her face. "Call me," she said.

"Yes, ma'am," I said, feeling sick.

When they left, I told Terrell to come out of the closet. I had to make him go home.

Terrell touched my shoulder. "I'm sorry for popping up and puttin' you in a tough situation. Are you okay?"

"No, please, just leave," I begged.

"I said I was sorry," he said, trying to pull me in his arms.

I shoved him away. "You ain't gotta go home, but you got to get the hell out of here."

He looked confused. "Why you trippin' out all of a sudden?"

My heart was racing. Suddenly, I felt the weight of my wrongdoing. "We can't do this."

"Do what? What are we doin'? It's not like we're humpin'."

"Just go, please."

He stepped away from me. "So what about the other night?"

"What about it?" I hated to treat him coldly.

"How you gon' play me like that?"

I toughened up and put my foot down. "Bye, Terrell."

"That's real cold, but it's all good." He strutted out the door like he was upset.

When I realized what I had done, I flopped down on my bed helplessly. I couldn't believe I'd given the boot to a winner. *It's for the best,* I thought.

⌘　⌘　⌘

Later on that night, Cammy called me. I mean, how could she resist the opportunity to make me feel bad? She gave me the first degree, making me feel awful. She talked down on me as if I had committed the great sin of adultery. "Don't fall for his game," she said. "What man wouldn't resist the opportunity to have a double-scoop of ass?"

"You're right, but it's not like that for the hundredth time. We're friends — that's it."

"Friends don't hide things in the closet."

"Okay, Cammy, you've made your point."

"I trust you, but I don't trust him. I think he's trying to have his cake and eat it too. It would make his day to have all the nookie he wants on a silver platter."

As she criticized me, I realized it was time to move on. Terrell was a done deal . . . although, his kiss made it hard to resist. I didn't know what it would take for me to completely get over him. While Cammy chewed me out, I clicked over to answer the other line. I started jumping up and down like those people on "The Price Is Right."

Rashard's voice sounded smooth and sexy. I didn't know what'd taken him so long to call but I was glad he did. I felt like he was the person I needed right now. *I'll be over Terrell in no time,* I thought.

At least I hoped.

6

Terrell hadn't crossed my mind in days and Rashard had a lot to do with it. We'd been hanging out and it was fun. It was exciting going to his basketball games and watching him shine; he was talented beyond imagination. Every game, he scored at will. One night, he set the record for most points and rebounds in a single game. I could understand why the NBA was eager to get him. There was so much hype surrounding him that there hadn't been any talk of our boys' football team going to state's. Rashard had everyone blown away, especially when he'd announced his decision to enter the draft.

I was a little overwhelmed too. I mean, every time I'd see or hear Rashard's name mentioned on TV, I'd go crazy. I was happy for him, and I hoped he remained grounded instead of letting the hype go to his head. So far, he seemed to be handling the pressure well.

One day at school, Rashard walked me to class. I felt like the world's luckiest girl as he carried my books. He wrapped his arm around my shoulders and looked at me. "I have a big game tonight; I want you to come," he said.

I smiled. "I'll be there."

"I appreciate your support."

We stopped in the middle of the hallway in front of my class. I saw Cammy peeping out the door, being nosy.

Rashard handed me my books and then placed a soft kiss on my cheek. "See you tonight," he said.

"Okay." I stood on my toes and kissed him on the lips. Cammy was my motivation.

Rashard grinned. "I like it when you go for yours."

I took it to the next level as Cammy watched us. I placed my arms around his neck and gave him another kiss. He put his hands on my hips and we kissed until the bell rang. People in the hallway had stopped to stare.

We laughed.

"I'll see you later," he said.

"Alright."

When I walked into class, Cammy was waiting for me at the door. "You lucky, heffa," she said, shaking her head.

I smiled and sat down at my desk. "Don't be jealous."

All hour long, I sat in class counting down the minutes till my weekend began. After the bell rang, I was out of there. I went home and got pretty for the big game.

⌘　⌘　⌘

That evening, I returned to school for the boys' basketball game. The gym was packed. There were people lined up outside fighting to get in while had the perfect seat. I couldn't believe all the pandemonium over one guy. The police had to intervene because of the frenzy. People were taking snapshots of Rashard during warm-ups. Unfazed by the flashing cameras, he remained focused while smacking on a piece of gum. His temples were moving a mile a minute and he looked all about business.

Rashard winked at me and I couldn't help but blush.

Somehow, Terrell spotted me in the crowd. He tipped his way up the stands, trying to avoid stepping on people. Then he squeezed his hot buns beside me. "How's it going, stranger?" he said.

I smiled. "How've you been, Terrell?"

"Missing you. Where are your girls?" he said, looking around.

"Everybody had their own plans."

Terrell looked on the court. "I didn't know you liked basketball."

I shrugged. "I came to watch Rashard."

Terrell looked at me. "Like the whole world minus the President, huh?"

"The only difference is I was personally invited."

He twitched his neck like a girl, trying to be funny. "Oh, excuse me, Miss Thing," he said.

"You're excused," I giggled.

"Don't tell me you diggin' him?"

"Why?"

He nodded. "You can do better."

"I think you're jealous."

He scrunched his forehead. "Ain't nobody jealous. I'll give him his props; he's definitely got game. I think he's gon' be a star when he goes pro." We watched Rashard dunk the ball backwards. I cringed because his head almost touched the rim.

"Damn, that boy got *ups*," Terrell said. Then he turned, facing me. "Real talk now. Friends are supposed to look out for each other, right?"

"Yes," I said, even though I felt he was hating.

"I'm only tryin' to look out for you because I know how dudes play games."

"Thank you, but I'm already hip to the game," I said.

Terrell stood up like he was leaving. Just then, I noticed the scratches on his neck. "Why don't you stay for the game?" I said.

"I gotta pick up Andrea from choir rehearsal."

A feeling of sadness came over me. "Terrell, what happened to your neck?"

He touched the welts on his neck. "Me and Andrea got into an argument."

"It looks like you got into a fight."

"You know how she acts when she doesn't get her way."

"I don't care. She has no right to put her hands on you."

"I'm tough; I can take it."

I shook my head. "You shouldn't have to take it. You need to put her in check."

"It's not gonna do any good."

"You want me to set her straight?"

"I'm a man; I can hold my own."

"If you say so."

Terrell touched my shoulder. "You be careful, though. I've heard about that cat," he said, pointing Rashard's way. "Ion't wanna have to hurt him for breakin' your heart."

"Don't worry about me," I said, getting spiffy.

"Okay." Terrell hopped down from the bleachers and headed out of the gym.

As Rashard dribbled the ball up court, I began having second thoughts. I was hoping Terrell wasn't right about him. Then I decided he was just jealous. At one point in time, Terrell was the big hype at school, but not any more.

I put Terrell out of my mind and enjoyed the rest of the game. On the hardwood, Rashard was putting on a show. All the oohs and aahs coming from the crowd proved that he was awesome. I was impressed. On one play, he had a dunk that brought the house down. All the brothers jumped out of their seats in amazement as Rashard did his thing.

When the coach took Rashard out of the game in the fourth quarter, he received a standing ovation from the crowd. He'd scored most of his 42 points off quick moves to the basket. I couldn't wait to get home and brag about him. It felt good to have someone special in my life for once.

Within a couple of weeks, I had totally fallen for Rashard. Falling for him was easy because he had it going on. Everything was going his way; he was voted to the McDonald's All-American game and the Slam Dunk contest. With all his success, I didn't understand what he saw in me. But he seemed to like me a lot because he wanted me to meet his family. I was excited, hoping he would make me his lady.

⌘　⌘　⌘

One evening, I showed up at Rashard's house like he'd asked me to do. When I arrived, he was outside playing basketball with his friends. I got out of the car and watched them battle head-on. A few of Rashard's boys had their eyes on me. They were staring as if they'd never seen a girl before.

"Dats all butta right there, homie?" a dark-skinned one said, checking me out.

I didn't pay them any mind as I focused my attention on Rashard. He weaved the ball between his legs while he talked trash to the boy guarding him. Then he made a move to the basket and fell awkwardly. He grabbed his knee, yelling in pain.

Everyone looked scared, especially me. My heart was pounding.

"You all right, homie?" one of his boys said.

Fortunately, he got up, and everybody breathed a deep sigh of relief.

"Yeah," I'm all right," he said, massaging his knee.

After that, Rashard and I went inside of the house. His home was decorated with fine African art and sculptures. The zebra-printed furniture was lovely too. Rashard kicked off his shoes at the front door and said, "That's what I get for being hard-headed. I didn't have any business playing with those scrubs." He led me in the kitchen and grabbed a Mellow Yellow soda out of the fridge.

"Is your knee going to be all right?" I said.

"It'll be fine. I'm gonna ice it tonight so it doesn't swell."

"Where's everyone?"

"I don't know. You want something to drink?"

"No thank you."

He burped loudly and said, "Excuse me."

After he finished his soda, he grabbed my hand and led me upstairs. When I realized he was taking me to his bedroom, I got nervous. I stopped at his bedroom door. "I don't feel comfortable being in your house without your parents home."

"Don't worry, my sister doesn't mind me having company. Besides, she's never home anyway because she works so much."

"So where are your parents?"

"My mom lives in Brooklyn and my pops is, hell, I don't know. Ten years ago, the faggot woke up and decided he didn't wanna be a father no more. I haven't seen him since."

"Sorry to hear that."

"I'm not worried about it."

"What made you move to Miami?"

"I was getting in too much trouble back at home." He lifted up his shirt and showed me a scar on his stomach. "See this cut?"

I shuddered at the deep ugly scar. "Yes."

"This is where I got stabbed. An inch higher and I would've been dead. Me and my homie was working the block when two snake mothafuckers tried to rob us. I refused to go out like a punk and let a mothafucker take what's mine. I wrestled the gun from one of them, but the other cat pulled out a knife and stabbed me."

"Oh my goodness! I'm glad you moved away."

"Me too because I wouldn't have met you," he said, pulling me into his bedroom.

He closed the door and blasted 50 Cent's rap song "21 Questions." Feeling nervous, I sat at the foot of Rashard's bed and flipped through a *Dime* magazine. I patiently waited while he went in the bathroom and showered.

When the water stopped, he walked in the room with a towel around his waist. The words "HE REIGNS" were inked on his back larger than life. I thought it was a cool tattoo.

He started rifling through his drawers for clothes to put on.

After a few seconds, I got annoyed. "Will you hurry up and get dressed, please?" I said. He was taking his dear time.

"Relax, ma," he said. "You act like you've never seen a naked man." His towel fell and I covered my eyes, catching a glimpse of his lizard. "Sorry about that, shorty." He went into the bathroom to get dressed. A few minutes later, he came out and sat on the bed close to me. "I really care about you a lot," he said, playing with my hair. "I wanna ask you something, but I'm afraid you may say no."

I gave him my attention. The thought of him asking me to be his girl had me excited. "I'm waiting," I said anxiously.

"Are you going to prom?"

"I don't know yet."

"I would like you to be my date if you don't mind."

"Sure," I said, trying to hold back my emotions. Although he didn't ask me to be his girl, I was content. I couldn't believe I'd been asked to prom by a superstar. I would've never dreamed it in a million years. At one point guys never looked my way. I felt on top of the world and I couldn't wait to tell my girls. Most of all I couldn't wait to see the looks on everyone's faces on prom night . . .

"Can I have some sugar?" he said.

I smiled and pecked him on the lips.

Rashard reached for the dresser and handed me a tube of hydrocortisone cream.

I looked at him, confused. "What'd you want me to do with this?" I said.

"Rub it on my back. This new tattoo is itching like a mugg," he said, lying down on his stomach.

I gently rubbed the cream on his tattoo. After I finished, he asked for a back massage. I massaged his shoulders as we talked.

"Who's your favorite team?" he asked.

"I'm not into basketball."

"You mean to tell me if I offered to fly you out to one of my games, you wouldn't accept my invitation?"

"Of course I would. What team would you like to play for?"

"I've always dreamed of playing for the Knicks, but if it doesn't happen, it's cool. I'm blessed regardless." Rashard started moaning.

"What's the matter?" I said.

"Your hands feel so good. Go lower."

I began massaging his lower back. "How's that?"

"Oh shit," he said.

"Watch your mouth, boy."

"I can't help it," he said. "When was the last time you had some?"

"Had some what?"

"Stop acting like you don't know."

"Oh, that?"

"Yeah that," he nodded. "I swear if I didn't know any better I would think you were a goddamn virgin."

"Whatever," I said, offended.

Rashard turned over and his thing was erect in his shorts. Filled with lust in his eyes, he looked at me. "Will you be my girl?"

When I said yes, he eased close to me and started kissing on my neck. Before I knew it, he had unfastened my jeans as I sat on the edge of his bed. He got down on the floor and started kissing my belly button.

I wanted him to stop because he was moving too fast. "Rashard, please . . .," I said, pushing his head away.

He started breathing heavily as he continued to press his lips against my navel. I scooted backwards, hoping he would get the point. Instead he pulled my hips back towards him and said, "Relax."

"I have to go."

"I won't keep you long," he said, reaching in his nightstand for a condom.

I turned my head as he slid down his shorts and put it on. Then he asked me to take my jeans off. "Rashard, I can't do anything with you," I said.

"What'd you mean you can't? Your period on?"

"No."

"Then what's the problem?"

"The problem is we don't even know each other that well."

He shrugged. "What is there to know?"

"Do you even know my last name?"

He looked dumbfounded. "What does your last name have to do with it?"

"You're missing the whole point," I said, zipping my jeans.

"Then what is it?"

"It's Johnson. Karla Johnson that is."

"Okay, got it," he said, kissing on my neck like he couldn't care less.

I pushed him away again.

"What is your problem?" he said. "Are you gon' let me hit it or not? I don't have time for games."

I hopped up, refusing to be a piece of meat.

"Okay, I'm sorry. Do you accept my apology?" he said.

I almost felt bad for him. "Yes."

He wrapped me in his arms and looked at me. "Since you aren't ready for that step, will you go down on me?"

"No," I said, offended.

Rashard got angry. "You must don't know who I am. Get the fuck outta my house!" he said, shoving me.

After he kicked me out of his house, I couldn't believe the way he'd disrespected me like a tramp off the street. I was through with him.

That night, he called me at 10:30 and apologized. I forgave him because I liked him a lot. His success caused me to overlook his arrogant ways.

⌘　⌘　⌘

For the next two weeks Rashard was pressuring me to sleep with him. Every conversation we had, he'd ask me when were we going to get down. I was becoming annoyed with his obsession with sex. I really liked him, but not that much. He thought I was making a big deal about it. On the contrary, I thought *he* was making a big deal about it. He thought I was playing hard to get because no other girl had ever made him wait so long. I'd thought about letting him be my first, but I was iffy. I wanted to get to know him better before we went all the way. One night, he got angry and hung up on me because I wouldn't sneak through his bedroom window and have sex with him. He hadn't called me since those last three nights. Every night, I'd sit by the phone hoping he'd call. There were times I regretted not sleeping with him because I didn't want to lose his friendship. And it bothered me that he wouldn't speak to me in school.

Eventually I got tired of waiting for him to call and drove over to Cammy's one evening. I was depressed as I rode across town listening to Justin Timberlake sing "Until The End of Time."

When I pulled up to Cammy's house, Andrea's car was parked in the driveway. I felt like leaving because I didn't care to be bothered with her. When I rang the doorbell, she opened the door. I felt like slapping her for scratching up Terrell's face. Instead, we hugged as if we were delighted to see each other. "Hey, girl," I smiled.

"You're right on time; we just ordered Papa John's."

"Sounds yummy."

"You don't sound too thrilled. What's wrong?"

"I'll be all right." I walked down the hall into Cammy's bedroom. Musiq Soul Child was on the radio and her room was a disaster. Every time her parents would leave out of town, she'd have the place in a shambles. "Where's Cammy?" I said, sitting on the bed.

Cammy stepped out of the bathroom, flat-ironing her hair. "Here I am. Give me the gossip."

I shrugged. "I don't have any gossip."

"Then you're not welcomed to stay," she said.

"Fine with me," I said, getting up to leave.

"I'm only kidding. Cheer up. It's nice to see you stop by. Ever since Superman flew into your life you act like you can't come over no more."

I sighed. "He can fall off a hundred-story skyscraper and splatter for all I care."

"Ouch," Andrea said.

"Where'd that come from?" Cammy said.

"He wants to do it."

"Do what?" Andrea said.

I looked at her coldly. "What do you think?"

"Oh you mean *it?*" Cammy said, pumping her hips.

"Yeah, it."

"I say don't do it," Andrea said. "He'll get over it and respect you more."

"I disagree," Cammy said. "He'll move on to somebody else who will give him what he wants — especially a guy like him."

"Then let him move on," Andrea said, shrugging.

Cammy shook her head. "If she really likes him then why would she let him get away, silly?"

"Okay," I said, holding up my hands. "Y'all are driving me nuts."

Andrea picked up Cammy's *Sister-to-Sister* magazine. "I say wait until you're married."

"What if she never gets married?" Cammy said, combing her hair. "Have you ever thought about that scenario?"

"No, and why wouldn't she get married?"

"Think about it," she said. "Look at the ratio of women to men. There aren't enough brothas to go around in the world. Especially not rich ones — the white women have them all. This is your chance, Karla. Rashard's fine, soon-to-be-rich, and available. You could be missing out on a good man trying to play hard to get."

"If he's such a good man he wouldn't be trying to get in her pants," Andrea said.

"That's not true. All men want it, even the so-called good ones."

"I don't think so, baby doll," Andrea said. "A good man will wait forever and that's the bottom line. My man is proof."

"Apparently you don't know your man very well."

I was embarrassed for Andrea. "Wow," I said.

Andrea looked as if she was getting ready to lose her religion. "Don't be mad," she smirked. "You, too, could keep a man if you learned how to keep your legs closed."

"That was low," I said.

"That's all right," Cammy said, looking at Andrea. "Your man ain't complaining."

"Keep wishing, heathen," Andrea said. "My man wouldn't touch you with a ten-foot pole."

I sat and watched them cut up like fools. I wondered what Andrea would say if she knew her man was digging me.

"What do you know about men?" Cammy said.

"I know enough not to let them use me up and throw me away like a pair of worn-out sneakers."

Cammy raised her eyebrows. "Oh, and I don't?"

Andrea flipped through the magazine, enraged. "Obviously not."

"Well, excuse me, Virgin Mary," Cammy said, twitching her neck.

I got aggravated with them arguing. Everything always had to be a debate. "I see right now I'm not going to get anywhere. Y'all can keep fighting if you want, but I'm leaving."

I walked out of Cammy's house feeling more confused.

As soon as I got home, I asked if anyone had called for me. No one had.

⌘　⌘　⌘

Our boys' football team won the state finals. Terrell shined big time. He had six catches for ninety yards and two touchdowns. That night, I wished I were in the mood to celebrate like everyone else at school. Cammy begged me to go out with her, but I didn't have the urge to do anything. I was still hoping Rashard would call even though I hadn't heard from him in two weeks. I'd been trying my best not to pick up the phone and call him. It was hard to get him out of my system, when every time I'd look up he was on TV.

As I sat on my bed watching *106 & Park*, Mommy peeped in. "I see you," I said, rolling my eyes.

She stepped in the room. "Why won't you come out this room?"

I shrugged. "I don't feel like it."

"Is there something we need to talk about?"

"Nope, I just feel like being alone if you don't mind."

She shut the door and looked at me. "You're not pregnant, are you?"

I was angry at the fact that she'd even ask. She and I had had serious feuds in the past about this. I could never forget the things she'd put me through because she didn't trust me. When I'd started high school, she'd take me to get check ups for fear that I was sexually active. I still couldn't find a place in my heart to forgive her. "No, I'm not pregnant; I'm far from that path," I said.

She smiled and made way to leave. "Good for you."

I stopped her before she left because I was tired of being bottled up in my own world of confusion.

"Yes, ma'am?" she said.

"Why are guys the way they are?"

"You mean selfish, inconsiderate, arrogant, stingy . . . the list could go on forever. Which type are you dealing with?"

I sighed. "All they care about is sex."

Her eyes stretched wide open. "You aren't having sex, are you?"

I looked at the floor and said, "No."

"Trust me, you're not missing anything. You ought to be proud of yourself. Keep your innocence for as long as you can because once you start having sex, you lose focus on everything." Mommy sat beside me and nodded. "Don't be naïve like I was. I've had my share of men whom I thought I could trust, but they were all dogs."

"Even Daddy?"

"He had his ways too. But, honey, let me tell you, don't be no fool. A lot of these young folks are having sex like AIDS don't exist; not to mention all the other diseases . . ." Mommy started talking about her dealings with guys in high school and how she got turned out at an early age. I was shocked that she told me those things. She really surprised me when she told me that she and Daddy used to skip school and spend all day bumping and grinding. "Your daddy put it on me," she laughed. Then she looked off into the distance as if she was remembering something sad. "Although your daddy had his ways, he still showed me what real love was all about. He wasn't like all the other guys who would get what they wanted and be gone. He made me realize that there are good brothers out there: brothers who are willing to serve a purpose in your life. All men aren't dogs, but you have to make them respect you."

⌘　⌘　⌘

After that talk with Mommy a week ago, I felt better. I felt like it was cool to be a virgin, especially after she'd warned me of all the diseases a person could catch. The one-on-one talk I had with Mommy was better than any conversation I'd ever had with my girls. At times my friends acted so immature that I couldn't take their advice. Their mentality was to side against each other; if one said hot, the other said cold. Sometimes I felt like I was stuck in a game of tug-of-war when it came to them. The other day was a prime example. Andrea wanted me to go to a gospel concert, while Cammy wanted me to go skating.

That night, I decided to hang out with Cammy; I couldn't see myself stuck in church on a Saturday night. When we walked into the skating rink, the music and disco lights sent me into a trance. I felt like I was at a '80s party as the DJ played "Don't Stop 'Til You Get Enough" by Michael Jackson.

I was ready to hit the roller rink when Cammy pointed out Rashard. I had to do a double take because I couldn't believe my eyes. Rashard had a hot Puerto Rican girl wrapped in his arms. His hands were on her booty as they skated in perfect motion. My confidence was shook because she had long silky hair; and to top that, she had nice curves.

"See, I told you he'd move on," Cammy shouted over the music. "That's how these guys are unless you're giving it up. There's always someone else who's willing to do what you won't do."

"So what are you saying? I should sleep with him?"

"All I'm saying is that you have to learn to let go and trust somebody."

Rashard and the girl started kissing.

My feelings were crushed. I sat down and watched them, hoping Rashard would acknowledge me. He never did.

Maybe Cammy was right.

⌘　⌘　⌘

Sunday afternoon, Cammy stopped at my house before she went to work. She walked through the front door hiding something in her Wal-Mart vest. "Where's your mama?" she said.

"In the kitchen, why?"

"I have something to give you."

"What is it?"

"I'll show you, but let's go to your room."

We walked past Mommy as she stood in the kitchen frying liver and onions. Cammy smiled and said hello. Mommy smiled back at her and then eyed me like she suspected Cammy to be up to no good. "How are you doing, Ms. Cammy?" she said.

"I'm doing fine."

When we got inside my bedroom, Cammy told me to lock the door. "Hurry up. I'm not trying to be late today." She pulled a DVD out of her vest and handed it to me. There was a butt-naked brother with a big penis on the front cover.

"Oh my gosh, Cammy! What do you want me to do with this?"

"Explore it so you can feel more comfortable with sex."

"I would love to explore a lot of things but this isn't one of them." I handed the DVD back to her, but she wouldn't take it.

"Just watch it. Gotta go." Cammy started to leave.

"Wait," I said, grabbing her arm. "Before you leave I need to tell you something."

"What?"

Gathering the courage, I blurted out, "Rashard asked me to go down on him." I felt embarrassed.

She laughed. "So what?"

I was surprised at Cammy's nonchalant attitude. "Don't tell me you would have done it?"

She stood there quietly for a second. Then she said, "I don't know; it depends on how much I like a guy."

"That's going a little bit too far, don't you think?"

"I mean, it's definitely not something you go around doing for everybody. Only tricks do that. You do it for your man and your man *only*."

Darn, I thought. I never knew Cammy was so loose.

She moved right along and said, "Where's my baby?" Then she opened the door and walked out of the room.

I followed her out. "I don't know. You know he stays in the streets."

"Do I," she nodded.

As I walked Cammy outside, Eric met us at the door. He pulled Cammy in his arms. They started smooching.

"Give me a break," I said, closing the door and leaving them outside. Then I went to my room and loaded the DVD. At first I was grossed out, but then I got comfortable, watching two people do it. It was interesting and it seemed like it felt good.

Fifteen minutes into the DVD, Eric barged into my room. "GOOD GRIEF!" he said. "Cuzzo is wearin' that thing out!"

I quickly turned off the TV. "Haven't you ever heard of knocking?" I fussed.

"I'm sorry. Put the flick back on. I wanna watch too," he laughed.

I shoved him. "Get out!"

"Wait a minute, chill. If a trick named Marie calls here for me, tell her I'm not home."

I shook my head at the way he disrespected girls. "I'm not lying for you."

Eric stopped at the door and looked at me. "Seriously, I hope you aren't doing those kinds of things."

I assumed he was referring to the porn flick. "Look who's talking."

He held up his hands innocently. "It's different; I'm a man."

"There's no difference."

"Like hell it ain't. Let me ask you this: would you rather give a beating or take a beating?"

"You can come up with all the analogies you want, but like I said, there's no difference."

He came to his senses and said, "You're right, there's no difference; but I don't want my sister doin' those things."

"You need to mind your own business."

He shook his head. "I don't wanna see you hurt."

"What about the girls you hurt?"

"Sorry to put it to you this way, but some of them ask for it. They give it up like they don't care, so what am I to do? But you can believe when I find me a good girl, I'm gonna make her my wife."

I was surprised. "I didn't know there was a soft side to you, boy," I said, impressed.

"Believe it or not, every man wants a good woman he can settle down with." He seemed uncomfortable. "I may sound soft, but keeping it real, you fit that category."

I didn't know whether to hug or slap him. Instead I told him to get out my room. I wasn't used to Eric being nice to me.

"One more thing before I go," he said, walking out the door.

"What?"

"You shooooo is ugly!" he said, mocking Shug Avery from *The Color Purple.*

I slammed the door and shouted, "Yo' mama!"

⌘　⌘　⌘

Two weeks before Christmas vacation, my acne resurfaced. There were so many bumps on my face that I could play connect-the-dots. Everywhere I'd go, I felt like people were staring at me. I hated going to school and showing my ugly face. I would've rather stayed locked up in a dark basement like One-Eyed Willy from *The Goonies.* In school, I tried avoiding people because of my breakout. For instance, whenever I'd see Rashard in the hallways, I'd take off in the opposite direction. I knew that if he saw my face, he'd probably vomit.

One day, I saw Rashard coming out of the gym. I made a quick turn into the restroom before he saw me too. I would've cried if he saw me. I took a good look at myself in the mirror. My confidence had fallen as low as the red tile on the bathroom floor. I refused to come out the bathroom until the bell rang in ten minutes.

As soon as the bell rang, I rushed down the hallway to get my books out of my locker. I thanked God the day was over. As I closed my locker and headed out the building, someone called my name. I ignored them and walked faster.

All of a sudden, someone grabbed my arm. "Hold up, girl. Where are you off to so fast?" Terrell said.

I couldn't look him in the eye because I was too ashamed of my acne.

"Is somethin' wrong? Why you lookin' down at the ground?"

"I have to go, Terrell," I said, shading my face.

He pulled my hand away from my face.

"Stop!" I said.

"What's wrong, Karla?"

I figured if I looked at him, I'd scare him away. I held my head up, waiting for him to react but he never did. If he was disgusted, he did a good job of hiding his emotions. "You happy now?" I said.

"What's your problem?"

I looked down again. "My face."

He lifted up my chin. "Is that why you gotcha head down?"

"It's uncomfortable and embarrassing."

"That may be so, but always keep your head up, Karla Johnson."

One of his friends called his name and he took off down the hall. After our exchange, I didn't feel so bad. Terrell had lifted my spirit as high as it could've soared. I wanted to run down the hall and give him a big hug. There was something about Terrell that made him irresistible.

7

I received good news to start off the New Year: I didn't have acne — I had chicken pox. I was happy when my dermatologist gave me the news. Thankfully, I was able to hide my polka-dot face behind Christmas vacation. I was so embarrassed that I refused to step foot out the house. With my luck, Terrell would've popped up and busted me with Calamine lotion all over my body. I'd already had to put up with Eric making fun of me, and that was enough. He'd pick on me and bring his friends to the house, seemingly on purpose. And like a creature, I'd stay locked in my room, starving all night until they left. I wouldn't have wished chicken pox on my worst enemy. Although my friends had the chicken pox before, neither of them came to see about me. They let me know the definition of a fair-weather friend, because that's exactly what they were while I was home suffering in pain. But looking on the bright side, I didn't break out near prom. Even though I doubted Rashard would take me now, I couldn't let that stop me. I prayed my blemishes and sores would be gone by then. And if not, I planned on caking on make-up.

⌘   ⌘   ⌘

After Christmas break, I refused to go to school the first week. That week out of school, I got caught up on all of my homework. During my days out of school, I watched fewer music videos. I was tired of watching fake people. Instead of watching TV, I added reading to my list of things to do to keep busy. I would read beauty-tip articles in *ESSENCE* and *Sister 2 Sister* magazine. I needed to know all the beauty tips before prom night, especially after Cammy called me bragging about her dress. She and Andrea were lucky because they had dresses and dates. On the other hand, I didn't have either because jobs and cute boys were scarce.

Realistically, I felt I could do without a date, but I couldn't do without a job. My folks had made it clear that if I wanted to go to prom, I had to pay for it. They expected me to pay for everything, even the $500-trip to Cancún. I knew it would take a miracle. I thought they were being unfair, but they were in for a big surprise if they thought I was backing out of prom.

One night, I sat in the kitchen and had a discussion with Daddy about prom. I wanted to know if he'd help me if I couldn't come up with the money in time. I thought it was the perfect time to ask, while Mommy was out celebrating the New Year with her sorority sisters.

"No," he said, while stirring a pot of rice.

"Why not?"

"We've already had this discussion, young lady. Besides I'm not too fond of my daughter going to prom with some guy."

"You have to trust me."

He laughed. "Trust me, it's not you who I don't trust."

I sucked my teeth and walked out the kitchen. Then I went in my room and shut the door. I wished my folks trusted me instead of thinking I was so gullible. In my opinion, they needed to get on Eric for slinging his thing around town. And what made it so bad, Daddy would hand him condoms like it was cool. As for me, sexual activity was forbidden. I mean, I'd get the first degree if I even mentioned going out with a guy. It was unfair. There were times I voiced my opinion that Eric needed to be chastised about sex, too, instead of patted on the back. But of course Daddy didn't see it that way. "Girls can get pregnant," he'd say. Then I'd have to remind him that they didn't get pregnant by themselves. Unfortunately, he'd brush me off and tell me, "It's a man's world."

That night as I lay in bed, the fire alarm sounded off. I rushed in the kitchen. Daddy had almost set the kitchen on fire trying to make rice. The pot of rice was smoking like a chimney. "I got it under control," he said, tossing the burnt pot in the sink.

I couldn't believe Daddy didn't know how to make rice.

"Will you boil your daddy some rice?" he begged.

"Do I have a choice?"

"No," he smiled sarcastically.

Daddy sat at the table and started reading his *SAVOY* magazine. I ended up spending my night in the kitchen. When the food was done, I fixed Daddy a plate of baked chicken, rice, and string beans. He put his magazine to the side and said, "Thank you."

You're welcome," I said. Then I fixed my plate and sat at the table. After I said my grace, Daddy looked at me.

"I forgot to tell you I got a phone call from the station; we had to book your friend at the jail," he said.

"Who?" I said, shocked.

"Terrell a.k.a. Mr. Trouble. If he wants to play ball, he's gonna have to get his act together. He needs discipline."

"Terrell is a good person."

"I don't doubt he is, but he needs to learn how to stay out of trouble. No college team is going to tolerate his actions off the field no matter how good he is. Where's the kid's father?"

"His dad's in the military. What did Terrell do?"

"The punk beat up his girlfriend. He's looking to add battery to his rap sheet."

"I don't believe it. Terrell isn't that type of guy; he wouldn't hit a girl." Suddenly, I couldn't care less about my spotty face. "Daddy, you have to let me go to the jail and see him."

"Not tonight."

"Why not?"

"Because I said so." He sounded firm.

"That's not right."

"That's life. Now eat your food and stop pestering me."

"I'm not hungry anymore."

He shook his head. "Instead of worrying about these knuckle-head boys, why don't you do something useful with your time like playing sports? You think if the Williams sisters had boys on their minds all the time, they'd be the greatest tennis players in the world?"

I rolled my eyes to the ceiling. "Whatever."

⌘　⌘　⌘

I stayed up all night worried about Terrell. I prayed he hadn't lost his cool and hit Andrea. I'd practically begged Daddy to let me go visit him, but he would've rather had me worry to death, knowing Terrell was my heart.

When I looked at the clock, it read 5:30 AM. I couldn't sleep at all. I wanted to call Andrea and give her a piece of my mind for having him arrested. That heifer knew Miss Sheila had been through hell and back to keep Terrell on a straight path. I doubted if Miss Sheila had the money to post his bail. I felt sorry for Terrell because there was no telling when he'd get out of jail.

⌘　⌘　⌘

At noon, I went to the jail. Daddy made a call to the jail from his office, and I was granted permission to go inside the jail. The jail lieutenant greeted me at the gate and led me inside of the jail. I hated coming to the jail because most of the inmates acted ignorant. As I walked through the corridor, they started whistling and yelling at me as if they were in heat. One of the inmates exposed his private part to me. I almost died. In one cell, the men started fighting like animals. That was the reason I worried about Terrell. He didn't belong in jail with a bunch of criminals. I was relieved when I saw him in a secluded cell. He was balled up in a knot, sleeping. I felt bad for him. "Wake up," I said.

He didn't budge.

The lieutenant knocked her club stick across the steel bars, alarming Terrell. "Wake up, sleepy head! You got company," she said. "Sweetheart, try and make it quick. We had a narcotics sting and they're on their way with the paddy wagon."

"Yes, ma'am."

Terrell looked at me through his sleepy eyes. He seemed surprised to see me. "What you doin' here?" he said, walking over to me.

"I came to see you. Tell me what happened."

He looked away. "I don't feel like talkin' about it."

"Well you better," I warned.

He sat back down on the filthy bench. "Just leave me alone."

"If you want to sit in there and pout like a big baby until your grandmother scrapes up the money to get you out of there, then fine with me." I started to walk away until he called my name. "I'm listening," I said, looking at him pitifully.

"I'm sorry," he said, cupping his hands around the bars. "I'm tired. I've been through a lot, you know."

"What happened?"

"I didn't touch her. She's the one that hit me."

"For what?"

"I wish I could tell you, but I don't wanna hurt you."

I stood there confused. "Hurt me how?"

"Look, I don't wanna talk about it right now."

"Well, excuse me."

"No harm intended." He shook his head. "I might lose my scholarship to USC," he said, sounding hopeless.

"Not if I have anything to do with it."

He gripped the bars tightly. "What do you have in mind?"

"I'm going to get you out of here," I promised. "Don't worry; I got your back."

He smiled. "I know you do."

I went to Daddy's office. He looked preoccupied, like he wasn't in the mood to deal with my problems along with his. I laid my troubles on him anyway. I pleaded for him to help Terrell, but he didn't seem interested in anything I had to say. I guess he figured he had more important things to do than helping somebody who couldn't keep out of trouble. After I realized I was talking to a brick wall, I walked out of his office upset. I felt like I had let Terrell down after not coming through for him. I couldn't go back and face him, so I left the jail in tears.

⌘   ⌘   ⌘

That afternoon, I stayed away from home long after Daddy got off work. I didn't want to look at his face. Everything always had to be about him. I didn't see the purpose of him being Chief of Police if he wasn't there to make a difference. In my opinion, he'd become a sellout.

As I sat in traffic waiting for the light to turn, more tears rolled down my face. Seeing Terrell lying in that cell hurt me to my soul. I felt sorry for him because he didn't have much. His mother was dead and he lived in those rundown apartments. *What else can go wrong for him?* I thought.

Finally, I went home after the gas ran low. Luckily, I didn't have any money because I would've driven far away. That evening when I walked in the house, I couldn't believe my eyes. Daddy and Terrell were sitting in the den watching TV. Terrell was snacking on a bag of Fritos as if he hadn't eaten in days. He looked at me and grinned his gorgeous white smile.

I looked at Daddy and he winked at me. I felt like I had the best daddy in the world.

⌘   ⌘   ⌘

My first week back to school, Mommy did my make-up because it was my first time wearing it. It was on point. My friends were excited to see me and they gave me compliments. I was excited to see my girls, too, but I wanted to slap Andrea. She had serious problems. At the beginning of the year, Andrea looked like a toothpick and now she'd picked up a lot of weight. Her face looked rounder and a shade darker. To top the list of bizarre, she'd wear clothes too big for her size to cover up her weight gain. The girl was acting stranger by the day.

One evening, I was in my bedroom working on my research paper about Oprah. The more I read about her, the more she inspired me. While sitting at my computer desk, my thoughts were interrupted when Cammy and Andrea invited themselves into my bedroom. Cammy sat on the bed and began going through my CD case.

All of a sudden, prom became the main topic of conversation. I didn't care to hear about prom because I didn't have a date. I'd crossed Rashard off my list a long time ago. I was shocked when Andrea said she and Terrell were still going to prom. After she'd had him arrested, I thought he would've learned his lesson. That was the reason I stayed out of folks' business. I'd made up my mind that the next time Terrell needed me, he could go to hell. I'd come to the conclusion that he and Andrea were made for each other because they were both NUTS.

As Andrea bragged about her and Terrell's matching prom attire, I wanted to vomit. She grabbed the bag of Doritos off my desk and began stuffing her face. After she sat there and ate half the bag, she went into the bathroom. A minute later, I heard her vomiting. I looked at Cammy to see if she'd noticed anything, but her lips were blabbing about prom, clueless. My head was spinning like a Ferris wheel; I wanted to disappear.

"Have you noticed anything differently about Andrea?" I said, interrupting Cammy.

"Yeah she's no longer anorexic."

I stared at her. "I think she's bulimic now."

Cammy shrugged. "I think she's fine. You can use a few pounds yourself, Slenderella."

"I'm serious," I said, concerned. "You're taking this matter for a joke."

"You sense everything, don't you?"

"I sure do."

"Why don't you sense the winning lottery numbers so we can have the bread for Cancún?"

"Whatever," I said, giving up on Cammy. She didn't care about anybody but herself. "I don't care what you say, Cammy. Something is wrong with that girl."

Andrea came out of the bathroom smiling. She could put on a front all she wanted to, but I knew something was going on.

"Girl, are you okay?" I said.

"Yeah, child," she brushed me off. "Do y'all have any more chips?"

I felt like saying, *Hell no! You just puked them all in the toilet.*

Black History month was at hand. The drama club acted out *Roots* by Alex Haley onstage in the school's auditorium. It was sad that folks had to act ignorant by talking and throwing things onstage during the performance. I didn't think my generation would ever appreciate the struggle our ancestors were put through. I bet if we had Mr. Clark from the movie *Lean On Me* as our principal everyone would've straightened up their acts. The only reason a lot of people had come to watch the play was to get out of class. I mean, no one was paying attention. Eric had his arm wrapped around Cammy's shoulders, not giving a care. Terrell was snoring on Andrea's shoulder. Rashard was acting ignorant too. He was cursing and laughing aloud during the play, but it was no surprise. He needed a reality check.

Rashard caught me staring at him and winked. I ate my pride and smiled back. Even though he'd dissed me, he was still cute. He got up and walked towards me. I had to blink twice to make sure he was actually coming my way.

He sat beside me.

Cammy looked at me and smiled. "You go, girl," she quietly whispered.

Rashard wrapped his arm around my shoulders and whispered in my ear, "Happy Valentine's Day, ma." Then he handed me a Hallmark card and said, "I miss you."

I got goose bumps when I felt his lips pressed against my earlobe. "You do?" I smiled.

"Hell yeah," he said, licking his lips. "Now tell me that you miss me too, but only if you mean it, shorty."

I couldn't help myself. "I miss you."

"So does that mean you'll still let me take you to prom?"

I couldn't believe it! Unable to trust my voice, I nodded.

"I can't wait. I'm gonna make it a night you won't forget," he said. Then he kissed me on the cheek. "Don't open the card until you get home."

I wanted to stop the play and let everybody know that Rashard had chosen me. I was star struck.

As soon as he left, Eric leaned over and tapped my knee. "What did he want?" he said.

"None of your beeswax," I said.

"I should go over there and bust him in the grill."

"My brother, why must you resort to violence?" Andrea said. "Just ask yourself, what would Christ do?"

Eric turned his body to face the back row. "My sister, why must you resort to speaking without being spoken to?"

"You are so rude," Cammy said, jabbing him in the side.

"I'm sick and tired of her trying to act so holy all the time."

"That's okay, I've been taught to turn the other cheek," Andrea said.

"Rashard only put his arm around her shoulders, for crying out loud," Cammy said.

"I don't care," Eric said. "He had no business coming over here trying to talk to my sister while I'm sitting here. It's called respect. It's a man thing; you wouldn't understand."

"Get over it. Your sister is a grown woman," Cammy said.

"I don't care if she was fifty. She's still my li'l sister and I dare him to try something with her."

"Shoosh," I said.

"You might as well scratch him off your list," he said. "All he wanna do is get in your draws. Why don't you talk to somebody your speed, like somebody in band? Don't be impressed because he can dribble a basketball. It doesn't mean he's gonna treat you right. . . ."

I ignored him while he went on and on.

"You haven't given him a chance," Cammy said.

"If you let the devil take an inch, he'll take a mile," Andrea said while rubbing Terrell's smooth chocolate face.

"Now I'll say amen to that," Eric said. Then he looked at Cammy. "You know for yourself all Rashard wanna do is beat."

"How do you know that?" Cammy said.

"'Cause I'm a guy and I know how guys think. If you had sense, you'd listen to me," he said, shaking his head.

"Just stay out of my goddamn business," I said.

"Yeah stay outta her business," Cammy said.

"I can't do that because she's slow like those kids that ride the short bus."

Terrell held his head up as if he was trying to figure out the commotion. Eric looked at him and said, "Will you please help me educate these young ladies about the games brothers play to get the draws?"

"All men aren't the same," Terrell said, yawning.

We all agreed with Terrell.

"Y'all can believe that lie if you want to," Eric said, laughing at us.

I ignored my stupid brother while he continued to rag on Rashard. I didn't know why he couldn't be happy for me.

Rashard was the first guy who had ever taken a serious interest in me, and he wanted to ruin it. But I refused to let him.

When I got home, I opened my Valentine's Day card. The poem was simple and sweet: *Roses are red and violets are blue, I hope you feel the same way about me as I feel about you. Love Rashard*

I couldn't get enough of reading it.

⌘   ⌘   ⌘

I started job-hunting right away. I was determined to go to prom and Cancún. My face had been glued to every help-wanted section in the paper for what seemed like months. Finally, all the searching paid off. I was offered a job at Family Dollar. The pay sucked but I figured by April I'd have enough money for prom and my class trip.

My first couple of weeks on the job was stressful. The white girl who I worked with had sticky fingers, and my register would always come up short. The girl stole so much that I had to keep my purse in the car.

One night after I got off work, I didn't know how to act after receiving my first paycheck. It felt good having my own money instead of running to my folks. For the first time in my life, I went to the store and bought my own deodorant, toothpaste, tissue, and pads. Cammy thought I'd lost my mind as she scanned my items in the checkout line.

I walked out of Wal-Mart feeling like an independent woman. I enjoyed working and making my own money. I'd put myself on a strict budget so I wouldn't spend all of my money on junk food. It was tempting, but when I thought about prom,

I knew it was worth the sacrifice. Besides, I refused to look like a Butterball turkey come prom night. I wanted to look like Cinderella on that night. After all, I had no choice when I was going with a dude of Rashard's caliber. The first time I told Cammy that we were going to prom, she seemed shocked, as if I wasn't good enough for him. I may've not dressed skimpy or had weave flowing down my back like her, but I still felt beautiful.

⌘　⌘　⌘

That night, I lay in bed unable to sleep. The howling wind and rain had me restless. As the storm grew stronger, the wind caused the tree branches to whip against my bedroom window. I hated that my folks were out of town. Eric had yet to come home and I was paranoid.

I freaked out when the power went out at eleven. When it came back on, I relaxed. A few minutes later, I heard a noise in the den. I got up and peeped in the den, but I didn't see anyone. "Is that you, Eric?" I yelled.

"Duh," he yelled back, turning on the lights.

I took a deep breath and walked in the den, which I regretted. Terrell was sitting on the couch. He had on a fresh Adidas sweat suit, while I looked a mess. I had on a raggedy T-shirt and a scarf tied around my head. I wanted to disappear into thin air.

"What's up?" he said.

"Hi," I said, heading back to my bedroom. I called Eric into my room.

"What?" he said, sticking his head in the door.

"What is he doing over here this late?"

"He's staying the night."

"You know darn well nobody's supposed to be in the house this late."

"Who's gonna tell?"

"I am," I said, slamming the door in his face.

I was upset that Terrell had caught me looking a mess; and I was more upset at Eric for not giving me a heads up. While I sat in my room mad, I heard them laughing and talking; they carried on for half an hour. I was anxious to know what was going on. There was no way I could stay locked up in my room while Terrell was in the house. I took off my scarf. Then I walked through the den and into the kitchen. To my surprise there was a dark-skinned girl sitting in the den. She was cute in her own way. I wondered if she had come to see Terrell. I got mad because I knew Eric was up to no good. Any time our parents left out of town, he thought it was playtime. He'd bring girls to the house and do whatever he pleased with them.

When Eric put his arm around the girl, I felt relieved. Terrell got up and came into the kitchen. "Y'all got any snacks?" he said.

I pulled out a box of Twinkies from the pantry.

Eric watched Terrell like a hawk from in the den. "No, man, we don't have any snacks," he said. "Now come outta the kitchen."

"You just don't want me around your little sister," Terrell teased him.

"You darn skippy," Eric said, kissing his company on the cheek.

"All I want is a Twinkie. Is that too much to ask for, dawg?"

I handed Terrell a Twinkie and winked at him. "Enjoy."

"Thank you. What's that you wearin'? You smell good, girl," he said, sniffing my neck.

I smiled. "It's called soap and water."

Eric rose up from the couch. "Terrell, come outta the kitchen before I have to lay you out!"

Terrell went back into the den. I turned off the kitchen light and said goodnight. My brother made me sick. He always had to mess up everything.

⌘　⌘　⌘

In the middle of the night, I had fantasies of Terrell lying next to me. I squeezed my pillow and pretended it was him that I was holding. As I fantasized him on top of me, a shadow appeared in the hallway. I sat up afraid to move. Then I heard a voice whisper, "It's me." Terrell tiptoed into my bedroom and closed the door.

I covered myself up. "Terrell, what are you doing?"

"I couldn't wait till your brother went to sleep so I could come talk to you. I couldn't sleep because you were on my mind." He sat at the foot of my bed.

"Did that girl leave yet?" I said.

"No, she's in Eric's room."

I shook my head. "You know what that means: one ho down."

He laughed. "How do you like your new job?"

"It's okay."

"What you doin' workin' when your folks got money?"

"That's what you think? They got money?"

"That's what I *know*. Your pops is the Police Chief, and your moms is a principal; add those two salaries up, and that's a lotta cheese, señorita."

"Whatever." I let Terrell think that lie.

He got comfortable and laid beside me. As usual, he smelled good. "Are you going to prom?" he said.

"Yes, I am."

"With who?"

"Rashard."

"Who? Say that again?" The moonlight shone on his startled face.

"I said Rashard."

"Tell me you're jokin'."

"I'm serious."

"I don't want you to go with him."

"That sounds like a personal problem to me. Besides you're taking Andrea."

"Not if you don't want me to. Just say the word."

"I'm not going to rain on her parade."

"Well, I'm not gonna pretend that I'm okay with you going with someone else. I wish I could give you the world like he can."

"I don't care about money. I can make my own."

"Go 'head on, Miss Independent," he said, snapping his fingers.

"If you don't know the meaning you better ask somebody."

"I admire a strong-minded female," he said, staring into my eyes.

I became bashful. "Will you stop looking at me?" I said.

We heard a noise in the kitchen. Terrell hopped up quickly. "I better get outta here before your brother kills me." He tiptoed to the door and then looked back and whispered, "I love you."

After he'd let the cat out of the bag, he took off. I wanted to run down the hallway and squeeze him in my arms. Instead, I sat in bed breathless, wondering if it was all a dream.

⌘　⌘　⌘

The next evening when I arrived at work, I sensed tension in the atmosphere. I felt like I was being watched. The manager stood over my shoulder all day. I thought it might've been because I was the only black employee. After I finished working with my customer, the manager led me into a small room. Although I hadn't done anything wrong to my knowledge, I sensed that I was in big trouble. I was right, too, because the next thing I knew, I was sitting face to face with a police officer explaining that charges were being brought against me. It wasn't just any officer; it was Officer Jackson.

I was embarrassed.

Officer Jackson escorted me out of the store in handcuffs. I was falsely charged with petty theft. I was so upset that I started crying like a baby. I couldn't believe I'd been arrested for something I didn't do. Now I understood what a lot of brothers went through. I didn't even get the opportunity to tell my side of the story. It wouldn't have mattered anyway.

Officer Jackson hauled me off in the back seat of his patrol car as if I were a criminal. As soon as we got up the street, he stopped his car. Then he took off my handcuffs and allowed me to ride in the front seat.

"I didn't take anything from those people," I said, rubbing my wrists.

"I knew that the second they told me your name. You know how many calls the department gets from that store about the same old garbage? Believe me, I've figured it out by now. The owner of the store is a redneck and he doesn't want blacks working in his store."

I felt angry and violated. "I don't know why he hired me then."

"Don't stress yourself, Karla. You have a lot to learn about life. Just keep your focus and stay in school so you don't have to be bothered with minimum wage jobs."

"Darn it. I really needed that job."

"I know a place you could work."

"Where?"

"My pops owns a meat market. He needs the help and the old man pays good."

My eyes almost popped out of my head. "What's good pay?"

"I'll negotiate for you."

"THANK YOU!" I said. "It was hard enough finding that crappy job back there."

⌘　　⌘　　⌘

A couple of days later, the storeowner dropped the charges. The proof was on video camera. When I got the news from Officer Jackson, I was relieved.

That day, I bought my prom dress. After all I'd been through, I felt good. Shopping eased my mind. I only wished that I could've done it more often. My prom dress was the bomb. I got brave and picked a white, strapless, beaded neck-line dress. I couldn't wait to rub it in Cammy and Andrea's faces, like they'd done me. At the time they knew I didn't have a date, which made it crueler.

After I left the mall, I drove to Cammy's house, but she wasn't home. Andrea's house was my next stop. When I got to her house, I wished I had kept driving. The girl had issues. I didn't get the chance to pull out my dress, because she broke down crying out of the blue. She wouldn't tell me what was wrong. I sat in her room trying to figure her out. Finally, she got herself under control and looked at me. "Have you noticed anything different about me lately?" she asked.

"No, like what?"

"My weight."

I couldn't crush her heart. "You've filled out but it's nothing strikingly noticeable."

"Terrell said I've put on a lot of weight."

"Who cares what he says or thinks? We always get caught up in caring what these guys think of us. If he doesn't accept you the way you are, then the heck with him."

She sniffled. "I never thought it would be me going through these changes."

"What are you talking about?"

"Nothing."

"Well, you look fine to me."

She turned, showing me her butt. "I'm spreading like a house."

"I think it's normal."

Andrea started crying again. "Why me?"

I put my arms around her. "Stop crying. You look fine." I felt awful lying to her. Andrea had blown up. I looked at her feet and they were swollen too. Her sandals made her feet look as if they were going to pop. I thought she needed to see a doctor to find out why she'd gained a ton of weight. It could've been an overactive thyroid gland like I'd studied in biology class last year.

I changed the subject and showed her my dress. "What'd you think?" I said.

She started crying louder.

"What's wrong now?" I said.

"I can't get into my dress anymore."

"You look fine. It's only your imagination."

"You think so?"

"I know so." I wanted to tell Andrea the truth but I was scared. Mommy used to tell me that it wasn't always good to speak the truth, and I never understood why until now. Andrea probably would've gone off the deep end and starved herself to death if I told her the truth. She seemed too fragile at the moment.

I put my dress back in the bag before I started more trouble. I thought it was messed up that I couldn't share the joy of owning my prom dress. As I packed up to go, Andrea sat on the bed and started stuffing her face with chocolate chip cookies. I doubt she realized how much she ate. She had become a snackaholic. The more I watched her, the more I worried about her. I was hoping she didn't eat herself to death.

⌘　⌘　⌘

When I got home, it wasn't a surprise to see Terrell. Lately he'd been spending a lot of time at our address. He and Eric were outside with a bunch of dudes. Dirt bikes lined the street as if there was a race on the horizon. As I rolled down the crowded street, everyone stood in the road. I blew the horn and they all moved as I pulled into the driveway. After parking, I sat in the car and watched Eric take off down the street like a nut.

When I got out of the car, Terrell rushed over. "What's up, Karla?" he said.

I covered my ears as the sound from the dirt bike engines popped. "I'm fine, thank you."

"You need to thank yo' mama," he said, looking at my backside.

I had on my favorite pair of shorts that made my booty look plump. "You are so crazy," I said, pushing him.

"'Ey, T, can I go next?" a tall, gap-toothed boy yelled.

"Go 'head, dawg, but I'm next." Terrell locked his attention on me again. "Are you gonna stay and watch me pop a wheelie?"

"You mean break your neck?" I grabbed my prom dress out of the car and his eyes got big.

"Lemme see your dress," he said, reaching for it.

I held it tightly and said, "Nope."

"Then be that way."

I shook my head and then shoved him. "Why did you tell Andrea that she's gaining weight?"

"Because it's true."

"Maybe she's going through something. Have you ever thought about that?"

He looked away stubbornly.

"I think you should —"

"I didn't ask for your opinion."

I was offended. "Well, excuse me."

"Can you do something for me?"

"Depends."

"I wanna take you somewhere tomorrow."

"I can't, Terrell," I nodded.

He grabbed my hand and said, "Pretty please."

"Terrell, I hate telling you no, but no."

"Will you trust me?"

I took a deep sigh. "Take me where, gee-whiz?"

"You'll see when we get there if you decide to go."

"Can you give me a hint?"

"Nope. So will I see you tomorrow?"

I gave in. "I guess so."

He smiled, seeming thrilled that he'd won me over. "Good, it'll mean a lot to me."

Eric snuck up on Terrell and put him in a headlock. "I already told you one time to stay away from my sister. My sister is off limits."

"I don't want your sister."

Eric held him in a chokehold as if they were in a wrestling ring. "Don't make me DDT your ass."

"Man, watch out," he said, fighting his way loose. They started slap boxing.

I went in the house while they acted like two children fighting over a toy.

⌘　⌘　⌘

The next day, I went to the mall and bought a cute dress. I wanted to look nice for Terrell. When I went to pick him up, he looked dressed for the street corner. He had on a hoodie and a pair of baggy jeans.

"Where are we going?" I said.

"You'll see." He stood at the driver's side door as if he were waiting for me to get out. "Do you mind if I drive?"

I opened the door and got out of the car. Daddy would've killed me if he found out. As Terrell and I switched sides, he studied me from head to toe. I was confident because my hair was cute, my toes were polished, and my legs were glistening. "Problem?" I said.

"Not at all," he smiled. Then he followed me around to the passenger's side. "Let me get the door for you." Terrell opened the door, then he walked around to the other side and got in the car. He adjusted the steering wheel and his seat. "You drive like an old lady," he nodded.

"I drive to arrive," I said, putting on my seat belt.

Even though Terrell was dressed in rags, he smelled good. He removed Usher's *Confessions* CD from the deck. "You ain't got no real music?" he said.

"Real music like what?" I said.

"Like some Li'l Wayne or Outkast?"

"Ugh, that's what you call real music?" I flipped through my CD case.

"Hand me R. Kelly," he said.

I handed him R. Kelly's *12 Play* CD.

He wiped it off and smiled. "This CD is a baby maker," he said, licking his chocolate lips. Terrell put on "It Seems Like You're Ready" and started popping his fingers. "Dis is da shizzle my nizzle!" He put the car in drive and we eased out.

As we cruised down the highway, Terrell kept me laughing while singing to the music. When his song went off, he looked at me. "I can remember I got my first piece of ass off that song. It was good even though I didn't know what I was doing."

"I'm glad you thought it was important enough to share."

"My bad. What song makes you reminisce about your first time?"

I shrugged, feeling self-conscious because I'd never done it before. "I don't know."

"Word? Maybe whoever that cat was didn't give you anything to remember."

"Maybe."

After driving miles across town, Terrell pulled into an old creepy graveyard. I thought he was going to take me to a place I'd enjoy. He led me to his mother's grave and knelt in front of her tombstone. I remembered him losing his mother to a heart attack in seventh grade. He came home from school and found her dead. Terrell went through a stage where he shut down and ran away from home. At the time, I didn't think he'd ever be able to recover from the loss of his mother. She was only thirty-seven years old when she passed away.

"You know, I haven't been out here since the seventh grade?" he said, brushing off his mother's dusty tombstone.

I kneeled down beside him and wrapped my arm around his shoulders. "Wow, I didn't know that."

"She was beautiful like you. I never understood why God took her away from me so early." His voice cracked. "You're lucky to have both of your parents, and you better appreciate them while you got them. People don't live forever."

"I do."

Although the cemetery gave me creeps, I was touched that Terrell had chosen to bring me. Especially since he hadn't visited his mother's grave since she'd passed away.

Terrell's eyes watered up. "I didn't mean to bring you out here and get all emotional."

"That's okay," I said, rubbing his back.

"If my mama were alive today, you're the girl I would wanna take home."

I laid my head on his shoulder.

"Even though I can't see her face, I feel like she's in heaven lookin' down on us right now," he said.

A teardrop snuck out of my eye. "Terrell, please stop; you're making me cry," I said, wiping a teardrop away.

Terrell got up and dusted off his knees. "We can go now. My job is done."

9

A month later, Terrell dropped Andrea like a bad habit. He claimed that it was time for them to go their separate ways. I truly believed it was because she'd gained too much weight. I bet he expected her to stay a size two forever. And like most guys, he didn't know the meaning of unconditional love. I thought he could've waited till after prom to break up with her. As bad as I wanted Terrell, I thought he was wrong. I didn't think it was necessary for him to kick her while she was down.

I could tell Andrea was hurting badly. Every day she worked out in effort to get her man back, but she failed to realize that losing weight was a gradual process. Although she'd exercise, it wasn't doing any good because her eating habits were terrible. She'd gobble a five-piece chicken box from Popeyes as if it was her last meal. It didn't take a rocket scientist to figure out the solution to her weight problem. It seemed like the only thing she'd lost was her self-esteem.

One evening, Andrea called me. She begged me to come over, claiming she needed to talk to me. She sounded emotional. I got in my car and flew to her house.

For an hour, I watched Andrea pace herself to Tae Bo. She was determined to lose weight. Sweat was flowing down her face in streams. Looking around, I saw a bottle of pills on Andrea's dresser; the label read Xenical. "Hey Andrea, what are these for?" I said, grabbing them.

She took them from me and put them in a drawer. "Nothing."

"Are you sick?"

"No."

"Then what is it that you needed to talk about?"

"Do you mind if I finish my workout?"

"Not at all."

I waited patiently while Andrea worked out. When I realized that I was missing *Jenny Jones,* I got antsy. Had I known Andrea was going to keep me waiting, I wouldn't have flown over to her rescue. I got dizzy watching her pounce around in a circle. Then all of a sudden, she passed out on the floor. I thought she was playing a joke on me. "If you don't stop playing around I'm leaving," I said.

Her body started jerking and flopping like a fish on dry land. I got scared and dialed 911 in a hurry. Andrea's folks weren't home and I didn't know what else to do. I was trembling. Time was valuable as I watched Andrea down on the floor, still flopping. I cried, hoping God wouldn't take my best friend away from me.

⌘　⌘　⌘

Andrea was hospitalized. She'd suffered from severe dehydration, which triggered her seizure. It was scary because she could've died. I thought Terrell was to blame for everything that she was going through. If it weren't for him dumping her, she wouldn't have been in that position. Images of her flopping on the floor were stuck in my head. There was no telling how long it would take for her to recuperate. I couldn't believe she'd let Terrell get the best of her. Even though I was disappointed in her, I was glad that she was doing okay.

Besides Andrea falling ill, the entire week was hectic. Cammy backed out of prom because she'd caught Eric at the mall with another girl. She was mad at me because she thought I knew about the ordeal. In my defense, I'd warned Cammy from the beginning of his doggish ways. If she hadn't given up her goodies, he probably would've respected her more. She was taking things hard too. Between Cammy and Andrea, I didn't know which of them had it the worst. I thought I had problems, but they had me beat.

One night, I called Cammy to see how she was doing. It was apparent she hadn't recovered completely because she'd missed three days of school and she sounded terrible. I could tell by the sound of her voice that she had been crying. I heard Shirley Murdock hollering in the background "I Can't Go On Without You." I thought listening to Shirley Murdock of all people was very depressing. I didn't know why Cammy was crying over spilled milk. I let her know that she needed to suck it up and get even. There was no reason for her to miss out on prom because Eric didn't know how to be faithful. "He'll get what's due to him," I told her. I'd meant it too. One day some girl that he really liked was going to come along and play him the same way he'd played Cammy. Until karma made its way around, I told Cammy she needed to get out of bed and turn on some Missy Elliot. As pretty as Cammy was, she could've found another date for prom in no time. I was going to make sure she found someone that looked ten times better than Eric. I doubted it would be a hard task, considering Cammy had more style than Mary J.

⌘   ⌘   ⌘

Two weeks later, I couldn't describe the feeling of having my girls over to my house like old times. Andrea was out of the hospital and Cammy was no longer confined to bed. They both sounded better since they'd decided to move on with their lives. Now our mission was clearer; we graduated in less than three months and college life was on our minds. We were excited about living in dorms, meeting new people, and pledging. Andrea was the only one who didn't seem optimistic about pledging. The only thing she was concerned about was finding a good church to join.

As we sat in the den, the mood shifted when Eric and Terrell walked in the house. I watched Cammy and Andrea's smiles turn into frowns. Eric and Terrell said hello. My girls looked at me as if they dared me to speak to those creeps. The atmosphere was full of animosity. To keep the peace, I gave Eric and Terrell the cold shoulder.

A couple of minutes later, my friends got up to leave, as if they couldn't stand to be in the same dwelling as their exes. I begged them to stay, but they didn't want to. They had serious grudges against Eric and Terrell.

Before they walked out the door, I pulled Andrea to the side. "What did you need to talk to me about that night?" I said. For the third time, she put it off for some reason. "Come on, Andrea, what is it?" I said.

She seemed embarrassed and afraid.

"You can trust me."

"Now isn't the right time," she said, walking away, head down. It bothered me that she wouldn't open up to me, just like it bothered me that Terrell wouldn't open up to me at the jail.

As soon as they left, Eric and Terrell zoomed their attention on *106 & Park*. They acted like two dogs when Beyoncé's "Crazy In Love" video came on. I thought it was cold that they didn't show any concern for Andrea or Cammy's feelings after they'd left. It was as if they didn't have a care in the world while my friends were in emotional ruins. I began to wonder if Terrell was the perfect guy I'd thought or just a selfish jerk.

"Man, if I had a girl like that I'd never cheat," Eric said.

"Tell me about it, dawg," Terrell said, high-fiving him.

"Keep dreaming," I said, feeling slighted.

Eric's cell phone rang and he seemed excited. "You're outside now? I'm coming," he smiled. He hopped up quickly. "She's here," he said.

"Who?" I said.

"None of your business."

Terrell got up and looked out the blinds. "She's okay, but she ain't all that, yo," he said, sitting back down.

I got up and looked out the blinds. There was a blond-haired girl sitting inside of a Mustang convertible. I rolled my eyes to the ceiling. "I can't believe you," I said, shaking my head.

Eric rushed outside. The shapely white girl got out of the car and hugged him. I watched Eric melt all over her. I hoped he was smart enough not to invite her inside, because I would've ratted him out for messing over Cammy.

I moved away from the blinds and sat back down on the couch. Terrell tried to strike up a conversation. At the moment, he was on my bad side, too. I ignored him while he talked to me.

"Hello, I'm talkin' to you," he said, waving.

"I don't have anything to say to you."

"Why you actin' all brand-new?"

"Uh, talk to the hand," I gestured.

"You know how I feel about you, and I'm serious."

"You need serious help."

"Don't insult me when you know I care about you." He leaned over close to me. "And I know you care about me too. Look at me," he said.

"No."

"Please."

I sighed and looked at him. "What?"

"Don't you?"

The phone rang, saving me from the truth. "Hey, Rashard," I smiled.

Terrell sat up and shook his head. I didn't care, though. I was excited to hear Rashard's voice, until he told me that he wouldn't be able to take me to prom. I wanted a strong explanation even though no excuse would've been acceptable. I felt like screaming through the phone: *How could you let me down at a time like this?* I had dreams of him and I walking through the door stealing the show. I wanted everyone to see that he had chosen me as his date. It felt like I'd waited my whole life for that moment.

I felt like crying, but I stopped thinking of myself when he told me that he had to fly to Los Angeles for an awards ceremony during prom weekend. I couldn't knock him for pursuing his dreams, even though he had crushed mine.

I couldn't let my girls know he'd backed out on me. No way on earth! They probably would've talked behind my back, but what hurt the most was knowing that no one expected a guy like Rashard to take me to prom. I wanted to prove everyone wrong, but instead he hung me out to dry. If I hadn't bought my dress, I wouldn't have pressed the issue. Besides, I couldn't back out on Cammy after encouraging her to go without Eric.

She would've killed me. For a minute, I considered going alone, because there was definitely no replacing Rashard.

After we hung up, I rolled my eyes at Terrell. Then I tossed the portable phone on the table.

"What's wrong?" he said.

"None of your business."

"He let you down, right? Don't worry 'bout it; he did you a favor, Karla."

"What do you know about treating someone right?" I got up and went into my bedroom. Terrell was the last person who needed to throw stones after the way he'd dogged Andrea. I would've been a fool to believe a word he said.

That evening, I sat staring out the window, wishing Romeo would fly in on a cloud and escort me to prom. It would've made my day.

⌘ ⌘ ⌘

My heart was crushed into pieces because Rashard had backed out on me. I'd been walking around school like a hopeless child. During lunch, the frustration grew because I had to listen to Cammy brag about her supposed new date for prom. A cousin of hers named Jasmine had planned to hook her up with some guy. I was so desperate that I would've gone with anyone.

I watched Hollis get up and walk towards our table. He sat down beside me. Cammy stuck her finger down her throat, pretending to vomit while Hollis wasn't looking.

"How are you beautiful ladies doing this afternoon?" he said.

Cammy smirked.

"We're fine," I said, being polite.

"That's good to hear." He leaned over in my space and looked at me. "I don't mean to disturb you, but I would like to know if I could take you to prom?"

Although Hollis was no Romeo, I felt honored. If he didn't have bad breath or a throwback high-top fade, he would've been all right. Maybe I was pushing it but he wasn't butt-ugly. I was about to say yes when Cammy interrupted.

"Too late, loser. Rashard already asked her. So, poof, be gone." She snapped her fingers.   Hollis got up and walked away like his heart had been crushed into a thousand pieces. Cammy started laughing while stuffing down a slice of pizza. "I can't believe Craig Mack Jr. had the audacity to step to you, can you?"

"Nope," I said.

I knew exactly the way Hollis felt.

1 0

On prom night, I dreaded putting on my dress, knowing I was going alone. Even though I was depressed, I managed to pull myself together and finish getting dressed. My hair was overflowing with long pretty curls and my make-up was perfect. As I stood in front of the mirror, I felt beautiful, but nothing could ease the pain of not having a date. *Why me*, I thought.

As I grabbed my purse off the bed, a pearl-white Lamborghini pulled into my yard. I stared out my bedroom window waiting to see who had hit the lottery in our family. As the doors rose into midair, I felt like I was staring at a car from out of the future. When Rashard stepped out of the vehicle, I felt faint. He looked as sharp as a switchblade dressed in a black tuxedo.

My parents watched me run to the front door yelling, "Oh my God!"

"What in heaven's name is wrong with you, child?" Mommy said.

"Okay, get it together," I told myself. Then I turned and looked at my folks. "Please do not embarrass me, you guys."

Daddy held up his hands. "My mouth is sealed," he said.

"You just make sure you're home at a decent hour," Mommy said.

When I opened the door, Rashard surprised me with a beautiful rose. His hazel eyes and juicy lips made me want to hump him on the doorstep. "Surprise," he said, giving me a hug.

"How did you make it back in time?"

"Anything for you."

I kissed him on the cheek, thankful that he'd come through for me. I couldn't wait till everyone saw me tonight.

Daddy snuck to the door; he seemed astonished. "Hey, you're, uh . . . ?"

"I'm Rashard," he said, shaking Daddy's hand.

"Yes! You're the ball player that's going pro."

I gave Daddy the eye and he backed off. "Goodnight, Daddy," I said.

Daddy was in awe. "You kids have a wonderful time," he smiled.

"Thank you," I said, closing the door.

Rashard opened the car door for me. "Thank you," I said.

"You're welcome, ma."

Tonight seemed too good to be true. I felt like I was dreaming.

When we got to prom, it was chaotic. Rashard's stardom was too much for me to handle. Folks would crowd our space and push me out the way, especially the girls. They'd surround him as if he was walking the red carpet at the VMAs. I got tired of it because his time belonged to everyone except for me. I was nonexistent. Although we'd come together, we went our separate ways.

I was thankful I had Cammy to keep me company through the night. It looked like she found her date in a backstreet alley. His shoes and clothes were busted. He and Cammy weren't matching at all. Her date had on more colors than a bag of Skittles. To add to the confusion, he had on a purple tuxedo, which was too small for his egg-belly. I knew Cammy didn't want to be with him. She was making herself miserable trying to fake it. I was embarrassed for her because Eric had a date from heaven while she had a date from hell. Eric's Caucasian friend had it going on; she looked as if she belonged on a runway in Paris. The girl had long brown hair, pretty green eyes, and perfect olive-toned skin.

On the other hand, Terrell had come to prom alone. I was curious to know why he didn't have a date. He couldn't have been turned down. That would've been impossible. Who could say no to Terrell? Especially when he was looking fly from head to toe. He looked handsome in his black three-piece suit, as he stood on the dance floor watching the girls dance to "Temperature" by Sean Paul. I was amazed when he started dancing to the beat; he had all the right moves. Although I felt angry and neglected, he put a smile on my face. I was happy to see someone enjoying the night, unlike me.

For most of the night, I sat at a table watching everyone else have a good time. I figured it could've been worse when Cammy darted across the room barefoot. She'd been dodging her date all night. Cammy crawled to my table and sat down. "Tell me if you see a tired-looking ol' man coming this way," she said, ducking low. "Where's Rashard?"

"I don't know and I don't care."

"What happened?"

"He's too busy enjoying the spotlight. I would've been better off staying at home. This is embarrassing."

"You're not the only one who's embarrassed. I'm here with a sweaty old fat man who smells like a jar of pickles."

"Why would you bring that old man with you anyway?"

"Because he paid for everything including the hearse we came in."

"You guys came in a hearse?"

"Yeah, and I think there's a body in the casket."

"You're kidding?"

"I swear it. Every time we'd hit a curb, I would hear *clunk!*"

I started laughing. "How old is he?"

"I'm ashamed to tell you, girl, he's fifty-six."

"Whoa! He may have a heart attack fooling around with you."

"Good!"

I laughed.

Five minutes later, I saw Cammy's date looking around the room as if he was lost. "There goes your man, Cammy."

He spotted Cammy sitting at the table and headed toward us.

"Where damnit?" she said, looking around the room, paranoid. As soon as Cammy saw him, she took off in the opposite direction, leaving me all alone. I thought it was a shame that I'd come to prom with Rashard and he was across the room all over another girl.

Terrell moon-walked off the dance floor and sat at my table. "Why are you sittin' over here alone? Where's your date?"

I looked up and saw Rashard place his hands on the girl's hips. The girl whispered something in his ear. Rashard grinned and licked his lips as if he was turned on.

I folded my arms, disappointed. "Terrell, go ahead and rub it in."

"What you said? I can't hear you?" he said, shouting over the loud music. He moved closer to me.

"I said: 'go ahead and rub it in.'"

He checked out Rashard too. "Hey, it's hard to keep your head on ground level when you got it like that, yo. There's talk that he's going as the number-one pick."

"Good for him."

"At least you have a date, unlike me."

"You made the choice to come alone."

"No, I didn't. You wouldn't come wit' me."

"You said that right."

"That's why I came alone. If I couldn't take you then I didn't care to bring anyone else." He changed the subject when he saw Cammy dash across the room barefoot. "What on earth was Cammy thinking when she brought that ol' school pimp wit' her?"

"She was trying to teach Eric a lesson."

"I'm sure she taught him a good one by robbin' the rockin' chair."

I laughed until I cried.

Terrell and I wound up sitting together the entire night. He kept me company while Rashard delighted in fame. Terrell and I had such a good time that I hadn't realized it was going on two o' clock. After I'd checked the time on his watch, I felt two hands grip my shoulders from behind. When I looked up, Rashard was standing over me. He and Terrell gave each other a cool handshake. Then Rashard looked at me. "I've been looking all over the place for you. Let's bounce."

I was hoping he would say that because I had to get home; I had a curfew to beat.

⌘ ⌘ ⌘

As we were riding, Rashard placed his hand on my thigh. "Where do you wanna go now, ma?"

"Home."

"But I didn't get to spend any time with you. I wanna make this night complete."

I had to make a decision quickly: *Do I break curfew or not?*

Rashard begged me to spend time with him so I chose to break curfew. But I had no idea that he meant spending time together in a hotel. He got out of the car and paid for the room before I could say no. It would've been nice if we had discussed getting a room before he had done it. Personally, I would've enjoyed a walk on the beach instead of being cooped up inside a germ-infested hotel room. There was no telling what kind of bacteria lurked between those hotel sheets.

Rashard flashed the room key in front of my face and turned off the ignition. "Let's do the damn thing," he said. Seeing that I hadn't moved he said, "Why aren't you gettin' out?"

"I don't want to stay inside of a boring hotel room while everyone else is out having fun."

"You can't worry about what everyone else is doing."

"Well, I think being cooped up in a hotel room is boring."

"A million things come to mind that we can do. I promise you, I'll keep you well occupied tonight," he said, kissing me on the cheek.

"Let's go to South Beach."

"You know it's impossible for us to go out and have our privacy. Look, tonight I'd like to be one-on-one with you. Besides, the room's already paid for and I can't get a refund."

"How much was the room?"

"A hundred and eighty-five dollars."

"Are you serious?" I couldn't believe he'd paid $185 for a room. Immediately, the word *shopping* came to mind.

"I'm not a cheapo, especially if I think a girl is worth it —
and I expect the same from her."

"What about what I want to do?" I said. The hard look on
his face let me know that he was fed up.

Rashard sucked his teeth and said, "Come on, we're wasting time." He got out of the car and opened my door, reaching
for my hand.

I didn't give in. "I would rather you take me home."

He sighed. "I didn't pay for a hotel room for nothing. Now
stop playin' and get out the car. I don't have time for this shit!"

I got out of the car.

"Thank you," he said, closing the door. "I can't believe
you're taking me through this hassle. You owe me some pussy
for putting up with your ass," he said, smacking me on the
butt.

At that point, I was disgusted. "I'll walk home," I said,
walking away.

"I ain't stopping you, bitch."

I gave him the finger and shouted, "Screw you!"

He hopped in his car and sped off.

⌘   ⌘   ⌘

I hated Rashard for leaving me stranded. I wished bad luck on
him, like a busted knee. Feeling lost and afraid, I headed up
the highway. The streets were dark and creepy. I didn't have a
penny to my name to call for a cab and I was too embarrassed to
call home. As I walked the streets, my feet were aching. I took
off my heels and continued full speed ahead. The pantyhose I
had on were shredding and the morning dew had caused my

curls to droop. I kept looking over my shoulder as cars passed. I prayed this was a bad dream and Rashard would reappear.

After twenty minutes passed, I realized that Rashard was long gone. I saw a group of thugs hanging on the corner drinking and smoking weed. I crossed the desolate street to be cautious. As I looked over my shoulder, I saw a black truck slowing up. I was terrified as it trailed me up the block.

"Hey, girl!" someone said. I ignored them until they yelled, "Stop!"

Out of fear for my life, I took off towards the gas station ahead of me. The person in the truck sped up too. I could hear the tires screech as they chased me.

"Stop, Karla, it's me!" a voice said.

I stopped when I heard my name. I peered in the truck as it pulled closer.

Terrell had a confused look on his face. "What'd you doin' out here alone?" he said. Then he parked at the curb and got out of the truck.

I stooped down to the ground gasping for air.

Terrell kneeled down beside me and started rubbing my back. "What happened?" he said.

I felt like crying. "It's a long story and I don't want to talk about it. Can you please take me home?"

"Did he hurt you? I swear to God I'll fuck him up."

"I said I don't want to talk about it!"

"My bad."

⌘　　⌘　　⌘

After Terrell pulled in my driveway, I gave him a hug. I didn't know what I would've done without him. "Thank you," I said.

"No problem. You know I gotcha back."

"How did you know where to find me? Were you following us?"

"Who me?"

"Yeah you."

"No, it was just a lucky coincidence."

A reflex caused me to kiss him on the lips. I wanted to get away after I realized that I'd kissed him. It was obvious he didn't mind because he leaned over and kissed me back. We started kissing and we didn't come up for air. His tongue felt warm in my mouth. I could taste his breath and it was on point. As we tongue kissed, I felt his hand climb up my dress. He rubbed the inside of my thighs, giving me a funny feeling. When he got close to my crotch, I got a grip.

"What's wrong?" he said, looking into my eyes seductively.

"We can't do this."

He shook his head. "We aren't doing anything wrong. I love you," he said, kissing me again.

"I love you too." Before I realized what I'd said it was too late — but the crazy thing was I meant it. "I have to go, Terrell," I said. I got out of his truck before things got hotter.

"Call me tomorrow," he said, backing out the driveway.

When I walked inside of the house, Daddy was lying on the couch half-awake. I was nervous because I was two hours past curfew.

"You're late, young lady. Where were you?" he said.

"I was sitting outside in the car talking to my friend."

He shook his head. "You know I'm usually easy going, but you better stop pushing my buttons. Now hurry up and get out of those clothes before your mama wakes up throwing a fit."

"Yes, sir."

I walked through the house and everyone else was sleep. Eric was laid across his bed in his prom attire as if he was wasted, and Mommy was snoring like a bear. When I walked into my bedroom, I felt like diving into bed. Instead, I went to shower, noticing a clear heavy discharge in my panties. I got upset because my body had never done that before.

⌘　⌘　⌘

Two days after prom, I never called Terrell. I was ashamed for letting the words *I love you* roll off the tip of my tongue. Whether I meant it or not, I was wrong for saying it. I wished that I had stayed home on prom night. It would've been better than a guilty conscience ripping me apart. If Andrea ever found out about that kiss, I knew she would've killed me. Although I'd let my emotions get the best of me that night, I had standards. I would've never done anything to stab my best friend in the back. We'd been through too much together: cried together, laughed together, shared secrets together, borne cramps together, and we'd cheated our way through trig together. I mean, if that wasn't true friendship then I didn't know what to call it.

One day after school, I sat in the bleachers watching the boys' track team practice. Andrea and I had made plans to meet at the track. Supposedly, she was ready to let out her big secret. I couldn't wait to hear what she had to tell me. I'd been baking in the sun for forty-five minutes. If it weren't for the half-naked boys' track team, I would've left.

When I looked at my watch, it looked as if Andrea had stood me up again. As I packed my things to leave, I almost lost my mind when Terrell ran out on the track without a shirt on. His chest and six-pack was chiseled to perfection. I crossed my fingers, hoping he wouldn't spot me in the bleachers. Since prom night, I'd been trying to avoid him. The more he was out of sight, the easier it was to forget what we'd done.

After he darted down the track, I quickly got up. Unfortunately, Cammy spotted me and came up the bleachers. Lord knows I didn't feel like being bothered. The girl had more issues than *TIME* magazine.

I took a deep breath and sat down as she talked a mile a minute. She was debating whether or not she should take Eric back. When she asked for my opinion, I told her that I was staying out of it. I refused to waste my breath on a stupid question. At times, I wished I could've charged a fee for listening to her problems — I would've been filthy rich. Cammy never seemed to realize that I had my own problems. For starters, I was curious to know why my body acted strange on prom night. Although I felt embarrassed, I cut Cammy short and asked her about the discharge in my panties.

She started laughing at me. "Who's the lucky guy that made your love come down?"

"What?" I said, confused.

"Am I speaking French?"

"Pretty much."

"Let me break it down for you nice and easy, hon. That was your body's normal reaction to sexual stimulation."

"For real?"

"In short he got you 'wet' or got you 'hot.' You feeling me?"

"Ew, that's nasty," I said, embarrassed.

"Well it's a part of nature. Now please tell me that you and Rashard got busy on prom night? I want all the details."

"Girl, we didn't do anything, so there's no need to get your hopes up high."

"You ain't no fun. Let it had been me, I would've tworked it on him," she said, winding her hips.

"I don't like him."

Cammy looked at me like I was crazy. "What do you mean you don't like him?"

"He's not a very nice person. Sometimes people let money and fame change them."

"What are you talking about?"

"Rashard is an egotistical asshole who thinks everyone is supposed to kiss his ass."

"Where is this coming from?"

"Don't worry about it." I left it at that because I didn't want to go into detail.

"Then who's the lucky guy?" she said, confused.

Just then, Terrell jogged up the bleachers.

"If he comes up here, don't say anything to him. Just ignore him," she said.

Terrell approached us, glistening in the sun like a chocolate treat. His shorts were hanging low, allowing me to see his ripped torso. All kinds of bad thoughts ran through my mind.

"What's good, ladies?" he said.

We pretended like he wasn't there and kept talking. After we ignored his next question regarding Cancún, he left. I felt immature playing Cammy's little game.

"About Cancún, are you going or what?" she said.

"I don't have the money."

"Your folks would give you the money if you asked them to."

"Child, please, no they won't; I know that for a fact."

"Then find yourself a job."

"I know this officer who promised me a gig . . ."

She looked at me, curious. "Doing what, may I ask?"

"Cammy, I'm not like you. The job is legitimate, comprende?"

"Call him, girl. What are you waiting on?"

Cammy was right; I needed a job.

When I got home, I didn't waste any time calling Officer Jackson. His wife answered the phone, giving me a personal pop quiz. If only she believed I wanted a job and not her husband, she could've saved both of us the stress. She hung up on me. An hour later, I called back and Officer Jackson picked up the phone. I was relieved. He assured me that I'd be working in no time.

All I could think about was sunny Cancún and the beautiful beaches. I'd be lying if I were to say I wasn't excited about spending three days in Cancún with Terrell.

11

Officer Jackson kept his word. His old man put me to work at one of his meat stores. I thought his old man would've had me stocking shelves and handling money. Instead, he had me getting my hands and nails dirty. Mr. Jackson had me taking out the trash and everything. I wasn't used to manual labor because the men at home took care of that.

When Mr. Jackson ordered me to package raw meat, I almost skipped out on him. He brought a whole pig out the freezer and cut off the poor little thing's head. I almost threw up. But the hard work was paying off: I'd made $290 over two weeks' time. After I earned the other half that I needed for my class trip, I'd planned on quitting. I was tired of dreaming of dead mammals and meat hooks. Each day I had to wonder what I'd gotten myself into. *Three days in Cancún had better be like three days in heaven,* I thought.

As I stood at the register, Terrell walked in the store and seemed shocked to see me. "Since when you started workin' here?" he said.

"Since two weeks ago."

"You like it?"

"I'd rather work at a morgue."

"You trippin', yo."

"It can't be any worse than looking at pig guts."

"You're the one who chose to work at a meat market. It's plenty of other jobs out there."

"Well, it's too late for that now."

Terrell got comfortable, plopping on the counter.

"No, you can't sit up there," I said.

"Relax, Mr. Jackson is cool wit' me. He always hooks my grandma up wit' free groceries. I think my grandma be breakin' him off too."

"Boy, you're grandmother is saved."

"That don't mean she doesn't get horny. Go see if Mr. Jackson got our chitterlings."

"Yuck," I shuddered.

"Yeah, like that funky attitude you be givin' me at school when you're around your friends. What's up wit' that, yo?"

"I don't have a problem with you."

"Just Cammy does, right?"

I shrugged. "I don't know, you'd have to ask her."

"That's okay, I'm good." He skipped the subject and smiled big. "Are you goin' to Cancún?"

"Maybe, maybe not."

"Come on, stop playin'."

"Yes, I am."

"Oooh wee, I can't wait to see you in a thong."

I set a hand on my hip. "And who said you were?"

"Oh, I'm not?"

Mr. Jackson stepped out the freezer, as I was about to get some straightening.

"Hey there, Mr. Jackson, you got those chitterlings ready?" Terrell said.

"Fresh as always, son." Mr. Jackson set the bag of chitterlings on the counter. "Grab your grandmother some vinegar and bleach. And if you need anything else grab it."

Terrell grabbed a bunch of items and then walked back to the counter. I started to ring up his groceries.

"Don't worry about tallying him up," Mr. Jackson said. "As soon as he signs his name to a big contract, he can pay me back."

"True that," Terrell said, bagging his own groceries. After he finished, he looked at me. "Take it easy up in here and call me sometimes," he signaled, walking out the door.

As usual, Terrell had made my day.

⌘   ⌘   ⌘

Another two weeks of hell passed. I received my second paycheck and quit my job. I felt bad for leaving Mr. Jackson, but a girl had to do what a girl had to do. The night before the trip, I couldn't get any sleep; I was too afraid that I'd miss the bus, which departed at 5:00 AM. I didn't want to take any chances when I'd waited four years for my opportunity to go to Cancún.

The next morning, I left the house at 4:30 AM and got to school on time. Four Greyhound buses lined the street. As I stood in line waiting to get on the bus, I got nervous because I didn't see Cammy. I'd never known her to be on time for anything, but today, she was pushing it. As the line moved, I saw her gold Nissan Altima cut the corner.

I was relieved.

Cammy and her cousin hopped out of the car, grabbed their things, and rushed towards the bus. Cammy had mentioned that she was going to sneak her cousin on the trip, but I never took her seriously.

When I got on the bus, my mood changed from good to sour. Rashard was on my bus and he was cuddled up with a Spanish girl. I'd thought Rashard could take Terrell's place, which was a big mistake. Even though Rashard was cute, he wasn't as fine as Terrell. Terrell had the total package: looks, brains, and heart. I wasn't only feeling that way because Rashard had spread rumors around school that I was a lesbian. What made matters worse, he wouldn't speak to me or even look my way at school. But I refused to let his ignorance get to me. I knew who I was. Hell, I knew that I wasn't any less of a woman because I'd chosen to wait.

As I got settled in my seat, Cammy and her cousin got on the bus. Cammy ran up and hugged me, but I didn't like the vibe I got from Jasmine. She seemed wild and ghetto. I could tell it was going to be an interesting trip.

After Cammy got settled in her space, she looked around the bus. "What's up with you and Rashard?" she whispered.

"Old news."

Rashard stood up and walked to the back of the bus, leaving his friend. I felt bad for her because she was in for a big surprise. I hoped he wouldn't mistreat her the same way he'd mistreated me.

Rashard and his clique started cracking jokes and farting in the back of the bus. The bus smelled like a dozen hard-boiled eggs. Everyone quickly opened their windows. Rashard was acting so immature that it was sickening. I hated his guts because he had become so cocky. Somebody needed to cut him down to size and teach him a good lesson.

I saw Eric and Terrell getting on the bus in front of us. Terrell had on a pair of shades, looking like Mr. GQ.

"Who is that?" Jasmine said, pointing at him.

"Don't even think about it, hon," Cammy said. "He's a zero."

Jasmine squinted through her fake blue contacts, which complemented her vanilla skin tone. "He looks like a winner to me."

"Beware, chile. Looks can be awfully deceiving. He's a full-blooded dog," she said.

"Then what about the one in front of him?" Jasmine said, pointing to Eric.

"He's off limits — he's mine."

Jasmine grinned. "That's okay — I want the sexy chocolate one anyway."

That heifer may have her eyes set on Terrell but may the best woman win, I thought.

⌘ ⌘ ⌘

When we arrived in Cancún, it was beautiful. The turquoise waters were clear and the white sands looked like grains of salt. After two days of sailing the rough seas from the port of Miami, everyone was ready to get off the ship. As soon as our ship docked, we acted like five freed hostages as we exited. Terrell looked like a beach boy in his swim trunks and flip-flops. He took off his shirt and rubbed on sun block. Jasmine almost lost a contact when she witnessed his body. I wanted to smack her face for looking at him. During the display, I couldn't help but blame Cammy for ruining my trip. I'd planned on spending time with Terrell, but Jasmine was the focus of his attention. There wasn't any doubt in my mind that she was loose. I knew

Terrell could sense it, too, which was probably the reason he followed her around like a puppy dog. It was hard not to get jealous when Jasmine had a body like the video girls. But one thing she lacked was class.

That morning, Cammy and Jasmine roamed the island in their two-piece bikinis, flaunting their bodies. Cammy had the decency to wear a sarong around her waist. On the flip-side, Jasmine let it all hang out. There were numerous times I'd caught Terrell lusting after her voluptuous body; his eyes stayed glued to her breasts, which were bulging out of a small, red-hot bikini top.

As we strolled the streets of Cancun, I watched Jasmine push up on Terrell. She took snapshots of him with her disposable camera. He acted as if he got a kick out of it too, posing like a player. Both of them were getting to me. It really made me upset when Jasmine handed me the camera. "Take a picture of us," she said. They walked underneath a beautiful palm tree and struck a nasty pose — Terrell had his hands on her booty, while she squeezed her breasts.

"One more," Jasmine said. Then she bent over, while Terrell stood behind her with his hands on her hips.

After I took the shot, I threw the camera in his face. "Oh, snap!" he said, covering his eye. "What the heck is wrong wit' you, girl?"

I pretended like I didn't hear him ask me that stupid question. I might as well have stayed home if it was going to be this way. I felt out of place because everyone was doing their thing while I was stringing behind them.

After hitting the town, we hit the beach. A couple of white women were lying in the sun topless. There was no shame in their game. One of the women stood up, exposing her breasts like there was nothing to it. Eric and Terrell turned into stone.

Jasmine took off her top too, sending us all into shock. The girl had lost her mind. She cupped her plump breasts and ran towards the water. Terrell chased her like a dog in heat.

Cammy looked at me as if she couldn't believe her eyes. "I didn't know my cousin was such a ho," she said.

"Well, now you know," I said, crossing my arms.

"I like it," Eric said, smiling.

Cammy put a hand on her hip and snapped, "Who the hell asked you anything?"

Eric took off his flip-flops like he was getting ready to head for the water.

"Don't you even think about it," she said, grabbing his arm.

Eric snatched away. "Why are y'all acting so uptight? Loosen up and have fun. That's what we're here for damnit." He grabbed Cammy and dragged her out to the water as she fought him.

"Stop!" she screamed.

Eric picked her up and threw her in the water, ruining her $90 perm. Before we came, I told her it didn't make sense to get her hair done.

Cammy got out the water, dripping wet. Eric had to run for his life or she would've ripped off his testicles. "You dumb son of a bitch!" she yelled.

As she chased him down the beach, I headed back to the ship. I refused to stand around and watch Terrell and Jasmine hit it off. They were out in the ocean splashing water at each other.

I was heartbroken.

⌘ ⌘ ⌘

The next day, I watched Terrell wait on Jasmine hand and foot. Jasmine had him doing things I would've never expected, like spending his pesos. He bought her a cute bracelet and a T-shirt. She had him under a spell. And it seemed like she had cast her magic spell on Eric too. Jasmine had on a pink thong that had him spellbound. Cammy was upset but she got what she deserved for bringing the tramp. She thought I was making it up when I told her that Jasmine was up to no good. Finally, she woke up and smelled the coffee. At that moment, we made an agreement not to speak to Jasmine for the rest of the trip. I doubted it mattered, because she enjoyed hanging with the boys.

On the third day in Cancún, I bought a cute purple bikini. I would've worn the one Terrell had bought for me, but he didn't deserve it. Besides I couldn't force myself to wear a thong; I didn't have the guts. After I'd bought the bikini, I felt like it was a waste because Cammy and I didn't hit the beach. We spent the day locked in a cabin gossiping about Jasmine.

That evening someone knocked at the door. "Who is it?" Cammy said.

"It's me," Eric said.

She rolled her eyes. "I do not feel like being bothered with him."

"Stop faking," I said.

Cammy walked out of the room and never came back in. I figured Eric had buttered her up because she forgot about our plans; we were supposed to go dancing with two nice-looking white guys we'd met during breakfast.

I sat in bed hoping the day would end. The fact that I had wasted $500 on the trip didn't sit well with me. I was so angry with Terrell that I could've kicked his ass. Then I realized that he wasn't even worth my time or energy. I had come to the conclusion that he was a dog like the rest of them. After I'd come to grips with reality, I refused to let my last day in Cancún go to waste.

As I sat in the room, trying to decide my next move, someone knocked at the door. I ignored it until the knocking turned violent. "Who is it?" I shouted.

"It's me."

"Who is 'me'?" I knew it was Terrell but I wasn't giving him any easy breaks.

"Just open the door."

I opened the door and put a hand on my hip. "Must you knock on the door like a fool?"

"Then you should've opened the door," he said, peering into the room.

"Jasmine isn't here, so bye." I tried to shut the door, but he barged in the room and laid across the bed.

"I didn't come here for her. I came to see you," he said.

"Did you dump her too?"

"First of all, she's not my cup of tea. I like a nice reserved girl."

"How come I don't believe you?"

"Because you think all guys are the same."

"Did you do anything with her?"

"Heck no!"

"Stop lying."

He sat up. "I swear on my mama's grave. Your brother hit it, though," he said, smiling.

I shook my head. "Well, you were sure sweating her when we first got here."

"I was only having fun since someone else doesn't know the meaning."

"Uh-huh, sure. You know you were trying to get some too."

He got up and walked towards the door. "Whatever, you ain't gotta believe me. I'm out."

"Just kidding. I believe you, gosh."

"Then don't play wit' me, girl. I don't fall for anything; I got very high standards."

When he opened the door, I didn't want him to leave. I was tired of being alone. For once in my life, I swallowed my pride. "Would you like to take a walk on the beach?" I said.

"Sure, why not?"

I grabbed a few towels in case we got our feet wet.

Terrell and I hit the beach. I had on my bikini with a sarong tied around my hips. I knew sooner or later, he'd ask me about the gift he'd bought for me. "I'm not ready for a thong yet," I said.

He laughed. "I'm sorry. I don't know what I was thinking."

"That's okay."

Terrell and I talked nonstop. He confessed that he liked me since middle school, which I found hard to believe. I refused to believe that he didn't have the confidence to approach me, like he claimed. As we walked on the beach, time flew. Darkness had crept up on us, but the moon and the stars shone bright. After our long walk, I spread a towel across the sand and we sat underneath a hut of palm trees. The night was warm and beautiful. I'd spoken too soon when I'd wished for the day to end. At that moment, I wanted it to last forever.

Terrell rest his head on my lap, staring into my eyes. "Did you mean it when you told me that you loved me?" he said.

I played it cool. "I don't know what you're talking about, boy."

"Stop fronting, yo."

"I plead the fifth."

"Now you wanna plead the fifth, huh?"

I took a deep breath. "If I said it then I don't remember," I lied.

"Well, I'm man enough to admit my feelings."

I sucked my teeth. "Whatever."

"That's the sound of a guilty conscience," he said, flicking my earlobe.

"Stop."

"Nope, not until you tell me the truth."

I got annoyed and flicked sand on him. It got in his hair and he flipped.

"Watch out, girl!" he said, brushing the sand out of his hair.

"Sorry, but I told you to stop."

"You're lucky I dig you." After he brushed the sand from his hair, he sat close to me. Then he planted a soft wet kiss on my neck. The kiss sent a tingling sensation down my spine.

I looked at him speechless.

"Did I do something wrong?" he said, breathing down my neck.

I remained silent.

"Did I?" he asked again.

"No," I nodded.

He moved closer to me and planted a kiss on my lips. That kiss turned into fifteen minutes of lip locking. Then things got hot. He unfastened my top. When I felt his soft lips on my breasts, I didn't want him to stop. I closed my eyes and laid down as he sucked on them. He took his time and treated each one of them with care. All of a sudden, I heard his zipper go down. When I looked down, his thing was hard. My heart sped up when he placed my hand on it.

"Don't be scared," he said, making me stroke it.

I could've screamed as I rubbed it slowly.

Terrell caught me off guard and slid his finger inside me. Even though I felt ashamed, I didn't fight it. It felt too good.

"How does it feel?" he whispered while fingering me.

"Good," I moaned.

Terrell stopped and untied my sarong.

I knew things had gone too far when he slid off my bikini bottom. "Hold on," I said.

"What's wrong?"

"I don't want to get pregnant."

"I'm not gonna get you pregnant. I know when to pull out."

When I relaxed, Terrell took off his shirt and climbed on top of me. As he prepared to make love to me, I got nervous. "Are you sure?" I said, worried. "Jenny Jones had a show on teenage pregnancy. All the girls who didn't make their partners use a condom ended up pregnant or with a STD —"

Terrell put his finger on my lips. "Shhh, let me do this." He tried to put his thing inside me but it wouldn't fit.

"Ouch, it hurts!" I cried.

"Sorry," he said, kissing my lips. Then I felt him go at it again.

I pulled up because it was too painful. "Wait."

"What's wrong?"

"I don't want to get pregnant —"

He seemed a bit aggravated. "I'm not gonna get you pregnant, I promise."

I eased all the way up. "I trust you."

"Then what's the problem?" he whined.

"I don't want my first time to be like this. I want rose petals and all the things that make a girl feel special."

He sighed. "I should've known you were a virgin. Y'all play these childish games."

I pushed him away from me. "Screw you."

"I'm sorry. I swear to God I didn't mean it. Do you accept my apology?"

"Yes."

He kissed my lips. "What about palm leaves?"

"I don't think so."

"That's cool. I'm not gonna force the issue. That's not my style. I love you, okay?"

"I love you too." I watched him massage his stiffy. "Will you stop?" I said, getting dressed.

"Just look the other way until I'm done."

"Done what?"

"Hand me a towel."

"Oh," I said, tossing him a towel.

After he was "done," he got dressed. "Soon as we get back home, I'm gonna buy a bunch of roses."

I smiled and kissed him. "I can't wait."

⌘   ⌘   ⌘

I got back to the room at 3:45 AM, and tiptoed through the door.

Cammy flipped on the lights and looked at me. "Where've you been, heffa? We were worried."

"I'm fine, as you can see."

"Oh my goodness, have you been a bad girl?"

"What are you talking about, Cammy?" I said, annoyed.

"You got hickeys on your neck, slut."

"I got bit," I said, covering my neck. Suddenly, I realized that my diamond pendant necklace was missing — the one that my grandmother gave me before she passed away. I looked around the room hastily.

Cammy studied my every move. "You got bit on your tits, too, huh?"

I looked at my breasts and saw the red marks. "Cammy, leave me alone, please."

"Nope not until you tell me who's the lucky guy."

Somebody knocked at the door.

"That's probably Jasmine," she said, skipping to the door.

Unfortunately, it was Terrell. He handed Cammy my necklace and then said, "Goodnight."

I felt like jumping into the ocean.

Cammy closed the door and looked at me like I was a dirty rat. "That explains it all," she said, tossing the necklace at me.

"Nothing happened."

"I'm sure you would tell me if it did."

"Trust me, nothing happened."

"Then I suppose a vampire sucked on your neck?"

"Cammy, please keep this a secret between us," I begged.

She folded her arms. "If you don't tell her then I will. That way she can move on with her life."

"You're right." At that moment, I wished that I'd never come on the trip. I'd planned on telling Andrea the truth if Cammy didn't beat me to it. Cammy lived for drama and she had a bad habit of exaggerating the truth. She would've made a hell of a writer for the *National Enquirer.*

Instead of sleeping, I watched the ocean from my cabin window. All kinds of thoughts crossed my mind, like should I throw myself overboard while I had the opportunity? Drowning would've been better than coming clean. After all, I knew Andrea had mad feelings for Terrell. I could visualize our friendship coming to an end. I would've traded a million bucks to erase what'd happened on the beach.

But even though I felt awful, I still wanted Terrell to be my first love. After all, he was the first guy who I felt I could trust.

1 2

Two days after the trip, I prepared myself a sentimental speech while sitting in class. I was hoping Andrea would forgive me, but it remained a mystery. As I watched the clock on the wall, it was moving too fast. I wasn't ready to face her next period. All kinds of crazy thoughts ran through my mind. I could see her spitting in my face. Although I'd prepared for the worst, it didn't serve as solitude. I prayed she didn't let a guy come between our friendship. After all, guys could be replaced while true friendship lasted forever.

As time ticked away, I regretted not picking up the phone over the weekend and telling her the truth. At least I wouldn't have to look her in the face and break her heart.

After the bell rang, I waited to meet Andrea in the hallway. Instead I bumped into Terrell, the last person who I needed to see. "Have you seen Andrea? I said, looking at my watch. "She usually meets me here before class."

He shrugged. "I don't think she came to school."

"No way, that's unlike her to miss a day."

"Well, shit happens." Terrell pecked me on the lips in the middle of the hallway. He had definitely lost his mind.

"Don't do that," I said, looking around.

He shook his head. "Who gives a shit?"

"I do."

Terrell leaned on the lockers and folded his arms. "Are you coming to my house tonight?" he said, looking into my eyes.

"I don't know yet."

"What are you so afraid of? You know I wouldn't do anything to hurt you."

"I'm not afraid."

"Then let me make love to you. I wanna be your first, so you can know how it's supposed to feel."

"You're a trip," I smiled.

"I'm for real. Am I gonna see you tonight or what?"

After the way he'd kissed and touched me in Cancún, there was no way I could resist. "Yes," I said.

Terrell snatched me and put me up against the lockers, kissing me hard. That time Cammy caught us as she walked out of her classroom. I could've slapped the daylights out of him for exposing us.

"What's up, Cammy?" Terrell said, holding me in his arms.

She rolled her eyes at us and kept walking straight ahead.

"Why is she trippin'?" he said.

I pushed him away. "Maybe because you're all over me like hot fudge on a sundae."

He laughed. "Don't pay her no mind. She's just mad because you look better than her."

"Flattery will get you nowhere."

"I'm serious," he said, pulling me close again.

I slapped his hands away from my hips. "Stop! You know we're all friends — show some respect." I got upset when Terrell wouldn't stop pulling on me.

My English teacher, Mrs. Walker, smacked him in the back of the head with her grade book. "Let that young lady go to class," she said.

Terrell let me go as he ducked her blows. "Okay, Mrs. Walker," he said.

"Thank you, Mrs. Walker," I winked. I stuck my tongue out at Terrell as Mrs. Walker dragged him down the hall like a rotten child.

Terrell looked irritated. "I got the roses!" he said.

Mrs. Walker smiled. "Oh, you got me roses, huh? How sweet."

I ran down the hallway to catch up with Cammy. I called her name but she wouldn't stop and talk to me. Finally, I grabbed her arm. "Didn't you hear me calling you? I said.

She pulled away from me and said, "Don't fucking touch me! I don't have shit to say to you, bitch." Then she kept walking.

I was shocked that she'd snapped at me. I mean, it wasn't like Terrell was her man, and besides that everything was cool between us a day ago. My feelings were hurt and I wanted to know what I had done to make her curse me out. Suddenly, it dawned on me that she must've found out about Eric and Jasmine's secret rendezvous in Cancún, and was taking it out on me. If that was the case she could go to hell because I'd warned her that he was a dog.

⌘　⌘　⌘

After school, I rushed home to call Andrea. I wanted to know the reason she wasn't in school. Usually, she wasn't the one to slack up. On the flipside, Cammy would've missed a day if she couldn't find anything to wear. I left a message on Andrea's answering machine.

Two hours passed and she never returned my call. My girl intuition led me to believe that Cammy had ratted me out. Anger led me to call Cammy, but she hung up before I could vent. I felt like choking her to death. Out of frustration, I called her back. That time the line was busy; I figured that she'd taken the phone off the hook. As I paced around my room, Terrell crossed my mind. I called him, hoping he'd know Andrea's whereabouts. Unfortunately, Miss Sheila told me that he wasn't home. Anxiety had me on edge as I waited for Andrea's call. In the process, I felt like riding to Cammy's house and paving the street with her face. At that point, I didn't doubt she'd opened her mouth and told what'd happened in Cancún.

That night, I began having second thoughts about sleeping with Terrell. But then, I couldn't resist the thought of us making love as I lay in bed waiting for his call. All I could think about was the way he made me feel in Cancún. I was ready to become a woman — but the night seemed to be slipping away.

When ten o' clock came around, I called Terrell, but no one picked up. I was furious because I felt like everyone had played me like a fool.

Finally, I got fed up and called Eric's cell phone. "Hello," he said.

"Where's Terrell?" I said, puffing mad.

"He can't talk right now."

"And why is that?"

"Because I said so."

"Put him on the phone, Eric."

"No."

Right then, I assumed they were up to no good. "The both of you can kiss my ass!" I said, hanging up. My blood was boiling. It made me upset that Terrell would rather hang out with his friends than be with me. Eric was on my bad side too.

When Eric walked in the house at 11:30, I attacked him out of anger. "I hate you!" I said. "You better not ever ask me for anything as long as you live!"

Eric stared at me as if he was in a daze. "Are you finished now?" he said.

"Hell no, I'm not finished! Why the hell is everyone acting so damn shady?"

"I take it you haven't heard the news?"

"What news?"

"Andrea's in the hospital."

I covered my mouth. "What happened?"

"She tried to have an abortion and ended up doing more harm to herself. The baby is still alive in her womb, but she's in a coma."

"Oh my God!" I said in disbelief.

I'd stopped breathing while Eric gave me the details. It felt as though God had snatched the breath of life out of my body. I was hoping that it was all a bad dream and I would wake up. I stood there waiting for Eric to tell me that it was a bad joke, but he never did. The tears welled up in my eyes. "How many months is she?"

"Four."

I was in complete shock. "Whose is it?" I said, crossing my fingers.

"Who do you think?"

It felt like my heart had been pierced with a knife. "Does he know?"

"Of course, we just left the hospital. He's really going through it."

"I can't believe it." I disregarded my feelings for Terrell and thought of Andrea. I thought of the times that she needed to talk to me. I started crying. I felt that I was the blame for what she'd been going through. If only I had torn down her guard, she probably wouldn't be lying on her deathbed. Eric tried to comfort me, but it wasn't working. I became hysterical. My folks came running into the den as I cried in disbelief. I found it hard to believe that I was the last one to find out the horrible news.

⌘　⌘　⌘

I skipped school to go to the hospital. I had a math test but I didn't give it a second thought. I wouldn't have been able to think if I didn't see Andrea. I had to see her for myself because I was in deep denial. How could I believe she was in a coma, let alone pregnant?

When I got to the hospital, I hoped for the best. Reality hit me when I saw her on a respirator. Her face looked pale and swollen. It frightened me to see Andrea with a tube through her nose. Death had never crossed my mind until I saw her lying in bed like a vegetable. I ran out of the room crying because I wasn't prepared to see my best friend that way.

Three weeks later, Andrea still remained in a coma. Every morning it was hard for me to cope. I dreaded having to wake up for school. At times, I dreaded waking up at all. I hadn't had a decent night's rest in weeks. I was scared that one morning I'd wake up and somebody would tell me that Andrea was dead. I'd never experienced losing a close friend but it was a thought that constantly haunted my mind. I felt like my world was crumbling down all at once.

One thing that's for sure was that when it rained, it poured. Cammy wouldn't talk to me for anything in the world. Sometimes I wondered how she was doing. I seldom saw her at school in the hallways, and when I did, she'd walk past me as if she didn't know me. I'd already accepted the fact that we may've never been friends again, but only because she preferred it that way. I'd tried calling her several times to patch up things, but she'd ignore my calls. After she'd hung up on me the last time, I'd made up my mind that I'd never call her again. After that, I cried every day.

At a time of crisis, it would've seemed ideal for everyone to come together. Instead, it was the complete opposite. Everyone was pointing the finger at one another instead of sticking together. Andrea's family was giving Terrell a hard time because he knocked her up out of wedlock. Eric and Terrell weren't friends anymore, either. My brother had it out for Terrell because he thought we had sex — thanks to Cammy's big mouth. Despite what everyone thought about Terrell, I supported him, but it was hard because I was disappointed at him. I was so depressed that I wouldn't get out of bed, except for school. I no longer looked forward to the weekends at all. Every day was a struggle. Graduation was right around the corner and I wasn't excited about it anymore. I wasn't leaving for Spelman without Andrea.

⌘　⌘　⌘

After school on Friday, I went to the hospital. Terrell was sitting in the room with his head buried in his hands. I wanted to hate him, but my heart wouldn't allow me. Even though he'd let me down, I couldn't hold it against him.

I cleared my throat to get his attention. When he lifted his head, I could see the bags under his red eyes. It almost looked as if he needed medical attention. "Are you okay, Terrell?" I said, touching his shoulder.

"I'm holdin' up." All of a sudden, he broke down in tears.

It broke my heart to see him lose his cool. I thought men cried in the dark, but I guessed not always.

Terrell wiped the tears from his face and looked at me. "They're gonna induce labor and take her off life support tomorrow."

"What? They can't do that."

"She can't stay hooked up to a machine for the rest of her life," he sniffled.

I could feel my own tears welling up. "They can't give up on her that fast."

"It's not up to us. Her peoples think it's best."

I got mad. "I'm not going to let them give up on her, and you better not either."

"I'm sure her family knows what's best. I don't know about you but I can't stand to see her like this. And even if she does pull through, she may never be the same again."

"You don't know that, Terrell. She can come out of this and be perfectly fine."

"Look, I don't mean to burst your bubble, but this ain't no fairy tale movie — this is real life, you know." Terrell grabbed a pair of keys off the table and left.

I sat at Andrea's bedside for hours. During that time, I spoke positive words in her ear. I didn't know if she could hear me or not, but I tried my best to encourage her to fight. I reminded her that graduation was in two weeks, and that fall semester at Spelman was around the corner.

"Please wake up," I said, rubbing her face. I began to feel hopeless as she lay there like a vegetable. Suddenly, I broke down when I realized that Terrell might've been right.

I looked up when I heard someone walk through the door. Cammy saw me and stormed out of the room. It was obvious that she couldn't stand my guts. I kissed Andrea's forehead and then gathered my things to leave. When I walked out of the room, Cammy was standing in the hallway with her arms folded. She wouldn't acknowledge me.

"You can go in there; I'll leave," I said, teary-eyed.

She walked in the room, giving me the silent treatment.

⌘　⌘　⌘

Early the next morning, I woke up with Andrea on my mind. My eyes were swollen from crying all night, but I'd accepted her family's decision to pull the plug. I started thinking about all the good times we used to have together. I could never forget the expression on her face the day she'd found out that she'd been accepted to Spelman on a full music scholarship. Her face lit up like the night her, Cammy, and I went to see B2K in concert freshman year.

As I sat on the edge of my bed, I couldn't picture a casket and flowers. I refused to believe she'd let doctors decide whether I lived or died if it were I lying in that hospital. Knowing her, she would've called a prayer meeting at her church.

I got dressed and rushed to the hospital. When I got there, Andrea's room was empty. All the flowers and get-well balloons had been cleared out of the room. I was in complete shock. Three nurses gathered around me as I panicked. When they told me that Andrea had been moved to Labor & Delivery, I sighed in relief. I took the elevator two floors up to her room. When I walked in, Andrea's family was talking amongst themselves. Everybody looked hopeless. Andrea's daddy was in a corner gazing out the window. I felt like I had to put an end to everyone's fear and doubt. I spoke my mind, even though I may've been out of place. In my eyes, they were making a bad mistake giving up on Andrea. Doctors weren't always right. Besides, I believed in my heart that God had the final say. I begged Andrea's daddy not to let the doctor induce labor."

He seemed decided. "Arrangements have already been made . . . I'd rather see my little girl resting in peace," he said sadly.

I reminded him of his sermon, the one when he'd preached "All Things Are Possible If We Believe." I found it ironic that he didn't want to hear it. "I don't mean to be disrespectful, but where's the faith you teach and preach about every Sunday?"

He looked angry. "Excuse me?"

"Damnit, how can I believe if you don't?"

He looked at me with fire in his eyes. "Young lady, you're out of place!"

"I'm sorry."

Everyone stared at me as if I had lost my mind.

I left before I started any more trouble. Although I felt like an idiot for cursing at a preacher, I was glad that I'd spoken my mind.

⌘　⌘　⌘

That afternoon, I went home and stayed locked in my room all day. I didn't come out to eat or anything. I probably could've survived off the bucket of tears I'd cried. I was angry with Andrea for attempting to have an abortion. I didn't think raising a child would've meant the end of the world. Sure, it would've called for a big sacrifice on her part, but not her life. I would've given her a helping hand. I was a true believer that folks made life harder than it is. It wouldn't have been hard for everyone to pull together and help raise the baby. It would've beat attending a funeral.

Nighttime had crept up while I lay in bed thinking. It began to rain. As the rain poured down, a creepy feeling came over me — the creepy feeling of seeing Andrea in a casket. I stiffened up when I saw a shadow lurking outside my window. I almost screamed for Daddy. But then I relaxed when I recognized the shadow. I opened the window and Terrell crawled in dripping wet. He took off his jacket and flopped on my bed.

"What are you doing creeping through my backyard in the middle of the night? Don't you know my daddy will shoot you, boy?" I said.

"He doesn't have to shoot me 'cause I feel like blowin' out my own brains. I swear I do."

"Don't say that. You're not the only one who's feeling down."

"I know but I feel like everything's my fault. After all, she's carrying my seed. I'll never be able to live with myself if she doesn't make it."

As he sat on my bed, emotions took over me, making me realize that I was still in love with him. "Why didn't you tell me?" I sniffled. "I trusted you."

"I didn't wanna hurt you."

"That's bullshit." I wiped the tears from my eyes.

He sighed. "I'm sorry, Karla. If I could go back and do it all over again, I would've told you. But the truth is we had no plans of keeping it."

"That's no excuse, Terrell."

I got up when he put his arm around me. "Please don't touch me," I said.

He stood up. "I know you're upset, but I do have some good news though."

"What?"

"I went out to the hospital today and —"

"And what?"

"Relax let me finish. Andrea's mother decided not to let the doctor induce labor."

I felt my heart speeding up. "Are you serious?"

"As a heart attack."

I felt relieved as I grabbed Terrell excitedly. "Thank goodness!"

Terrell stared at the floor, looking dazed. "Yeah, I hope she pulls through."

Suddenly, I felt bad for the way I'd acted. "I'm sorry," I said.

"It's okay; I understand that you're hurt." Terrell hugged me and then crawled out the window.

After he left, I couldn't stop the tears from falling.

⌘　⌘　⌘

Two weeks later, graduation day had crept up. Although it was supposed to be a day of accomplishment, it felt like a nightmare. I figured I wasn't the only one who felt that way. At the ceremony, Cammy stared into space as if she was completely out of it. I wished I'd known what was running through her mind. It felt awkward not having her to talk to anymore. I missed both of my girls a lot. I never thought a day would come when Cammy and I couldn't stand each other. After kissing her ass, I was sick of her childish antics. I'd become as stubborn as her, although she was the one who didn't want to be friends.

After the ceremony, I joined my folks at the Olive Garden. Of course, Eric had to be selfish and go with Cammy's family instead of celebrating the night with us. I tried my best not to spoil the night even though I didn't feel up to celebrating. I had too many other things on my mind, like Terrell. I was concerned because he never showed up to graduation.

My mother looked at me and smiled while reaching for a garlic bread stick. "Baby, cheer up. You should be excited about what you've accomplished."

"I'm not happy."

"You'll be fine once you go off to school. Going to college is like starting a new life, baby. You'll meet new people, new friends . . ."

"I'm not going," I mumbled.

My mother almost choked on her bread stick.

"What the hell do you mean you're not going?" my daddy said, patting her back.

"I'm not going to Spelman; it's as simple as that."

"Then where do you plan on working? McDonalds or Burger King?" he said. "I think Taco Bell may pay a few more extra pennies."

I let my daddy do all the talking. I'd already made up my mind that I wasn't leaving without Andrea.

"Where do you plan on living?" my mother said, clearing her throat.

"I can make it on my own."

They started laughing at me. "You're joking, right? You can barely keep a steady job," Daddy said.

"Yes, I can."

"I can't believe this child. Talk to her, Norris!" my mother yelled.

Daddy leaned across the table and looked me in the eye. "Baby girl, listen to me. It's hard out there unless you plan on depending on a man to take care of you. And if so, all he's going to want you to do is keep his house clean and his bed warm."

"I don't need a man," I said.

"If you don't go to school then you're not living under my roof. It's my way or the highway," my mother said.

I scooted away from the table and got up. "Fine with me," I said, walking away.

My daddy stood up and yelled across the room, startling everyone in the restaurant. "What about the police academy, baby!" he said. "You're guaranteed health insurance and great benefits!"

I kept walking, not giving his option a second thought.

1 3

Two days later, the situation between my parents and me had come to a boil. I was tired of my mother telling me what to do. Out of spite, I decided to leave home. Monday morning, while my folks were at work, I made my move. My mother had pushed my buttons for the last time. Graduation night wasn't the only time she'd threatened to kick me out. She'd done it before, and I was tired of it. I packed my things without hesitation. After I finished packing, I imagined the looks on their faces. A *take that, sucker* feeling had come over me.

That evening, I found myself standing at Miss Sheila's front door. My pride wouldn't let me go back home. I would've rather slept in my car. As I stood knocking at Miss Sheila's door, it made me angry to think of all the fun things I'd missed out on in high school. My mother's distrust issues made life hell for me. I had to suffer because she got pregnant in high school. If it hadn't been for Daddy lending me a little leeway, I wouldn't have been able to go to prom or Cancún.

All of a sudden, my mind became consumed with the past. I remembered the times she'd embarrassed me — like when she'd take me to get check-ups and threatened to beat me to death if I ever got pregnant. My word was never good enough; she had to hear it from a gynecologist. Every time I'd visit the doctor, I cried because I felt violated. I couldn't cope with a stranger feeling my breasts and sticking a cold metal object in my vagina. As I looked back on my childhood, I was happy to be out of my parents' house, and I didn't plan on going back. It would've been a cold day in hell before I went back home. I was thankful that Daddy had signed for my car, because if not, I would've left it parked in the front yard.

After a couple of minutes, Miss Sheila opened the door. Usually, I would've been scared, but this time I was emotional and I had to let everything out. I told her that I had fallen out with my folks and that I needed a place to stay for a couple of days. I knew I needed more than a few days, but I didn't want to push it.

Miss Sheila gave me a shoulder to cry on. She let me know that I had a place to lay my head for as long as I needed. I didn't pass up on her offer.

I took my things out of the car and got settled in.

That night, Miss Sheila cooked a big meal although we were the only ones there to enjoy it. Terrell was in Texas visiting his father. I felt like I was home when she fixed me a plate of southern fried catfish, garlic mashed potatoes, string beans, and macaroni and cheese. I could've definitely gotten used to her home cooking — but I wasn't used to rodents; a rat ran across the kitchen counter and I screamed.

"They don't bite," Miss Sheila said, unfazed.

After dinner, I washed up and headed to bed. I slept in Terrell's room, while he was out of town. I slept like a baby, too.

⌘　⌘　⌘

The next morning, I woke up to the smell of homemade buttermilk biscuits. Cracker Barrel Restaurant didn't have anything on Miss Sheila. After I ate breakfast, I headed out the door. I went to a temp agency to find a job. It seemed as if I'd gone to the busiest temp agency in town. The place was jam-packed. People needed jobs badly. I began filling out paperwork regarding my work history and education. I didn't have much to fill out, because I'd only had two jobs, neither of which had lasted over a month. My lack of work experience haunted me. Luckily, I had an agent who went the extra mile and made sure I didn't leave without a job. After receiving job placement, I was so excited that I hugged her neck.

"Good luck," she said, seeming surprised.

"Thank you!"

I walked out the place with a smile on my face, thanking God for blessing me with a job.

⌘　⌘　⌘

A week later, I was working. My persistency landed me a rinky-dink telemarketing job, soliciting timeshares. My ego was bruised on my first day at the job. I was called every curse word from A to Z. One man told me to stick the vacation package where the sun don't shine, but not in such nice words. I wanted to quit, especially when he called me a nigger. After that experience, I was afraid to call anybody else's house. When I told the dark-skinned girl who was sitting next to me what'd happened, she started laughing.

"Get used to it, girlfriend. Most of the white people are rude," she said, batting her fake eyelashes.

"Wow," I said, preparing to make another cold call.

Throughout the day, I took more abuse. By the end of the day, I'd only made one sale, which was to a half-deaf old lady.

After I got off work, I went to the hospital. Even though Andrea was a vegetable, I felt as though she could hear me. I told her about my first day on the job, and that I wasn't leaving her side no matter what. I meant it, too. I didn't care if I had to solicit vacation packages for the rest of my life. I didn't think I would've been a true friend if I were to leave her side. I believed if I stayed at Andrea's side, she'd keep fighting. I promised her I'd keep my end of the bargain as long as she kept fighting. College was no longer a thought.

⌘　⌘　⌘

Another week passed and Andrea was still hanging on. I made it a priority to visit her every day after work. One evening, I bought dinner at the cafeteria and watched TV in her room. As I ate, I filled her in on my life and the latest gossip at work. "It's worse than a soap opera, girl, which is why I keep to myself. I don't have time for drama, and you know black folks can keep up some drama," I said. "Hopefully after this year, I'll have enough work experience to get a better job. Every day I have my ups and downs. One minute, I'm doing well and then the next, I feel like I want to give up . . ." As I talked, I nodded off. I was half asleep when I heard Eric's voice. I looked up and saw him and Cammy walk through the door. I grabbed my things and left the room. I assumed Cammy didn't want to breathe the same air as me.

Eric followed me down the hall. "Where do you go at night?" he said.

"Why?"

"Look, everybody's worried about you, including me."

"I'll be fine. Miss Sheila is letting me stay at her place."

"Why don't you come back home and stop acting ignorant?"

"I'd rather die."

"You can't stay with Miss Sheila for the rest of your life."

"I'll be on my feet in no time."

"I hope you don't think working at Ding Dong Telemarketing is gonna get it."

"How did you know?"

"I got chicks that keep me well informed."

I nodded. "It's not Ding Dong Telemarketing, it's Done Deal Telemarketing for your information."

"Like I said, Ding Dong Telemarketing, because that's where all the ding-dongs work. Go to school, Karla," Eric said, slowly backing away. "You need some education."

⌘　⌘　⌘

Two weeks later, Eric left to attend college at Florida State. I didn't get to see him before he left town. One day he called me from Tallahassee in an uproar about how fine the girls were at FAMU. He was more amazed that some of them knew his name. I told him he'd better be careful because some girls were scandalous. Eric had a promising career in football, if he stayed focused and didn't become distracted. I would've hated for him to get stuck with a baby. He also told me that Cammy was leaving at the end of the month to get settled in Atlanta for fall semester. It seemed like I was the only one who hadn't forgotten about Andrea. Terrell seemed unconcerned too, because he was still in Texas as if he didn't have a care in the world. I couldn't imagine leaving her side even though things were strenuous for me. I wasn't bringing in any money. Last week, my paycheck was $198.63 after taxes. I knew if I wanted my own place, I'd have to work two jobs. I'd put in applications at places like Taco Bell, Burger King, and Target, but no one had called me back yet. With the economy being bad, I realized I had to be patient. I'd sell newspapers on the street corner if I had to. There was no way I could go back home and suffer the words *I told you so*.

One evening, I picked up groceries after I left the hospital. I tried my best to contribute around the place. I was afraid Miss Sheila would get tired of me, although, she appeared to enjoy my company. To my advantage, we seldom crossed paths because she worked nights cleaning hotel rooms at the Marriot.

When I got to the apartment, Terrell was stretched on the living room couch watching *Martin*. I was surprised to see him, because it seemed he'd been gone forever.

Terrell seemed shocked to see me too. He was staring at me as if he'd seen a ghost.

"I take it that your grandmother hasn't told you the news?" I said, closing the front door.

He sat up. "Nope, she didn't tell me anything. I didn't know whose stuff that was in my room. What's goin' on?"

"What do you mean, what's going on?"

"I mean, why aren't you home?"

"I have my reasons."

Terrell followed me into the kitchen and helped me put up the groceries. "Did you fall out wit' your peoples?"

"Yes," I said, sitting at the table.

"What happened?"

"It's a long story."

He took a seat across from me. "I got time."

I told him what'd happened.

Terrell looked at me, disappointed. "Trials are gonna come but you can't let nothing stop you from pursuing your dreams, Karla."

At that moment, he sounded like Andrea. For a second, I thought she was sitting across from me. I was spooked out.

"Are you okay?" he said, flashing a hand across my face.

"Yes."

"Oh, you had me worried for a second." He took a deep breath. "I'm leaving for school in the morning."

"Are you really?"

"Yes."

"Are you excited?"

"Heck, yeah. I wanna make somethin' of my life. Most of the cats around here my age ain't doing nothin' wit' their lives. They're content wit' sellin' dope and robbin' —"

I ducked for cover when I heard loud gunshots outside.

Terrell shook his head, unfazed by the gunfire. "See what I'm sayin'?" he said.

After it stopped, I sat up. "Yes," I said, trembling.

"I wanna make my granny proud of me. I'm gonna be somebody one day; my granny ain't gon' ever have to clean up anymore more hotels. I just wish my moms were here to see me go to college. You're lucky to have both of your parents."

⌘　⌘　⌘

Terrell departed at 8:15 AM on a flight to Los Angeles. Last night we stayed up till the break of dawn reminiscing. We were able to recall every hit song that came out during middle school, like TLC's "No Scrub" and Sisqo's "Thong Song." We'd even gone back as far as elementary school when Immature and Shai were hot. I'd slipped up and admitted that "If I Ever Fall in Love" by Shai made me hot for him in elementary school. Those were the good ole days, we'd agreed.

After Terrell left, I'd already begun to miss him. His pictures and trophies spread throughout the place didn't help any. All they did was make me cry. I may've ended up missing Cammy, too, even though we were on bad terms.

As I stared at Terrell's senior picture hanging on the wall, it seemed like everyone was disappearing out of my life one by one. Then the harsh reality hit me that everyone had grown up and started going their separate ways in life. I thought I would've been excited to be out of high school. That was a big joke. Now I wished I could've gone back to the days when I didn't have a care in the world, except for having a boyfriend like all the other fast-tailed girls. Deep down inside, I craved the day when everybody would let go of their grudges so we could be friends again. I knew it may never happen, so until then I was willing to hold on to the memories of the times when Cammy and I were friends, Eric and Terrell were buddies, and Andrea was strong and healthy.

⌘ ⌘ ⌘

One night when I went out to the hospital, I brought a brush and some grease to do Andrea's hair. If Andrea knew the way her hair looked she would've had a fit. I wish I could've brought her something to wear also. I was tired of seeing her in the same old blue rag. I was used to seeing her in beautiful dresses with flowers. I didn't believe she would've just let herself go even though she was five months pregnant with a baby bump.

After I finished doing her hair, she looked like a doll. As I sat on her bed, Cammy walked through the door. Once again, I packed my things up to go. Breathing the same air as her was too hard.

"You don't have to leave," she said.

"I was leaving anyway." I walked out of the room.

Cammy followed me into the hallway. "I'm leaving tomorrow afternoon," she said.

I didn't know whether to cry or do cartwheels. "Oh, okay," I said.

"I didn't want to leave without saying goodbye." Cammy hugged me and I was shocked. "I'm going to miss you guys," she said. "You better take care of yourself."

"I will."

"If you decide to come, I better be the first to know."

"You will be; I promise."

She smiled and hugged me again before walking back inside of Andrea's room.

It would've been easier to accept the fact that Cammy was leaving, if we hadn't spoken to each other. As silly as it sounded, I didn't want her to leave. I almost wished she had walked out of my life without saying goodbye. Now it was going to be ten times harder for me to stop crying.

14

I started working a new job at IHOP. Ever since I started, I was able to save up more money; but if it weren't for good tips I'd be in the poorhouse. My only objection to the job was the crazy working hours, from 6 PM to 3 AM.

One night as I cleaned off a table, a few jerks walked in the door. Rashard and his boys were talking loud and acting ghetto. I prayed I didn't have to wait on them. After all this time, I still hadn't found a place in my heart to forgive him. Anything could've happened to me that night; I could've been hauled off into a backstreet alley and raped. I hated that bastard. I bet he thought he was Mr. Big Stuff ever since he signed an eight-million-dollar deal with the Clippers and received a Nike deal reportedly worth forty million dollars. I didn't understand why jerks like him made all the money, while teachers made peanuts. It was clear to me that the world had misplaced priorities.

We were short of staff, so I waited on Rashard's table. Immediately, he harassed me, making sexual comments about my ass. He and his friends acted like a bunch of hoodlums. Management didn't have the heart to ask them to leave. Rashard had too much clout for his own good. I brought them water and silverware. Every time I turned my back, they yelled, "Waitress!"

The fifth time they asked me to refill their drinks, I couldn't resist the temptation of getting even with them for making my night a living hell. I repented after I spat in each of their drinks. If they had any good sense they would've known not to mess with people who served their food.

When I brought out their food, they complained their orders were wrong. I took their plates back into the kitchen and then re-took their orders. I never would've thought I could have so much patience. The second time I brought out their orders, Rashard complained that I had put mustard on his cheeseburger when he asked for mayonnaise. The third time I came back, he complained that his French fries were cold. It was apparent he wanted to give me a hard time. He was doing a terrific job. I brought him out hot fries. Before I could leave, Rashard asked for another refill on his Sprite. I sighed and grabbed his cup for a refill. When I returned to the table, he had a big grin on his face.

"I may leave you a big tip for your southern hospitality," he said, taking a slurp. As I walked away, he called me back. "I'm not finished talking to you, missy," he said, picking up the dessert menu. "Me and my partners here would like some dessert." He closed the menu and then looked at me. "Since we're on the topic of dessert, has anybody popped that cherry yet, or you still saving it for marriage?" he said.

His boys burst out laughing.

I almost snapped, but I kept my composure because I needed my job.

Everyone placed their orders for dessert except for Rashard. Finally, he looked at me as if he was ready to order.

"What would you like for dessert?" I said pleasantly.

He licked his lips perversely and said, "I'll have a slice of your cherry pie."

I wanted to smack the grin off his face. "We don't have cherry pie."

"I'm looking right at it," he said, sliding a wad of money across the table.

"That's two grand," Rashard said. His boys looked at him as if he was crazy.

The money was tempting, but I looked at him pitifully. "You can't afford a girl like me."

"You wanna bet? I'll double it."

"Man, you better not pay four gees for a piece of ass," the dark-skinned one said.

The plump one shook his head and felt Rashard's forehead. "Are you a'ight, man?"

Rashard placed a second wad of cash on the table. "Come to the bathroom with me," he said, sliding out of the booth. "It's all yours if you do."

I looked at him and didn't budge. "I wouldn't sleep with you for a million," I said.

His boys looked surprised and started laughing. "You've lost your magic touch, Sensei," one of them said.

I walked away from the ignorance. Five minutes later, I brought out their desserts and placed them on the table. As I walked away, Rashard smacked me on the butt. I turned and knocked the hell out of him. Rashard looked shocked, as a co-worker had to subdue me. Everyone in the restaurant looked startled, including my supervisor who standing at the register. The uproar made him run across the room and yell, "You're fired!"

Although I lost my job, I felt vindicated.

⌘ ⌘ ⌘

When I got inside of my car, I cried like a baby. I wasn't up for the hassle of finding another job. The thought of it made me sick. I wiped my face with a napkin. Then I took a look at my face in the mirror. My eyes were red and puffy. I fixed my rearview mirror and then strapped on my seatbelt. I jumped when I heard a loud noise on the roof of my car.

Rashard had startled me.

I let down my window angrily. "You fucking idiot!" I yelled, putting the car in reverse.

"Stop!" he said.

I stomped on the brake. "What the hell do you want?"

"I'm sorry I made you lose your job."

I hit the gas and he jumped back.

"Will you stop before you run me over?" he yelled, hitting the window.

I stomped on brake again and looked at him. "What?"

"Damn, calm down, shorty." Rashard took a deep breath. "I just wanted to say I'm sorry for all I've put you through. You didn't deserve it."

"No shit"

"Everybody makes mistakes." Rashard tried to hand me his number. "If you ever need anything call me, okay?"

"That's okay; I'll pass," I sniffled.

"With no strings attached," he said, sliding his number in my shirt pocket. Then he reached out his hand as if he were calling a truce.

I placed my hand in his, glad that he was man enough to apologize.

"Take care of your biz, shorty, and stay sweet," he said. Then he jogged back inside of the restaurant.

A big smile spread across my face. The gentle side of Rashard was charming. I never would've thought there was a kind side to him; it was hidden underneath his huge ego. I eased out of the parking lot on a good note with Rashard, but losing my job at IHOP had me depressed. If there had been a cliff in sight, I would've driven off of it.

Tears filled my eyes as I drove the highway. I decided to go past my parents' house while in the area. Daddy walked inside of the house as I passed. I wanted to jump out of the car and squeeze him. I never realized how much I needed my folks until I'd fallen on hard times. For once, I put myself in their shoes; if I had children I would've wanted the best for them too. Ironically, "Dance With My Father" by Luther Vandross came on the radio, reminding me of Daddy and all the times he held me in his arms like I was his angel. Unfortunately, that tune had changed.

He closed the door and I kept riding like I didn't know him.

On the way to Miss Sheila's place, I bought a newspaper to look for a new job. I hated the thought of having to look again. Just thinking about it, made me depressed. But I refused to feel sorry for myself.

I grabbed my purse and got out of the car, locking my doors. All of a sudden, I felt a hard object forced to the back of my head.

"Bitch, you move and I will blow yo' mothafuckin' brains out!" a deep voice shouted at me.

I froze and prayed for my life. My hands were trembling. The man snatched my purse and took off down the street. I thanked God for sparing my life, as I watched him almost get hit. I shook my head, wondering why we robbed from each other. Hell, I was trying to make it too. Going back home came to mind as tears filled my eyes. But I felt as though I couldn't turn back now.

⌘ ⌘ ⌘

The next morning, I went to the DMV office to get a duplicate license. Luckily, I didn't have many valuables on me last night; I only had my license, make-up, and a dollar worth of change in my purse. After I left the DMV, I went to the hospital. Andrea's daddy was in the room talking with the doctor. I gave them privacy and stood in the hallway. After thirty minutes, the doctor left. I tapped on the door and walked inside of the room. Andrea's daddy had his head down. I wanted to know the 411.

He looked at me sadly.

Right then, I knew bad news was ahead. "Is everything all right?" I asked.

Andrea's daddy stood up and fixed his coat. "They're inducing her labor and taking her off life support this week," he said, walking out the door.

I looked at Andrea lying in bed. I couldn't even think.

When I got home, I stayed up all night like a zombie. I couldn't rest with the thought of losing Andrea. Maybe I was in denial, but I believed she'd pull through. Nothing could get me to think otherwise. I had something special that everyone else had lost: faith.

That night, I called Terrell to let him know the doctor was supposed to induce Andrea's labor. I couldn't believe it when he told me Andrea's family didn't want him in the picture. He claimed they didn't want him to be a part of the child's life at all. And they had the nerve to consider themselves Christians. As Terrell fed me the 411, I could sense that his heart was broken. He blamed himself for everything. I'd never heard Terrell sound so down, except for when he lost his mother. The more he talked, the more he began to scare me. I feared he'd go off the deep end. I couldn't deal with another tragedy. We stayed on the phone for a couple of hours. I didn't want to be alone and neither did he.

⌘　⌘　⌘

The next evening, I called to make sure Terrell was all right. There was no answer. I'd spent all day trying to get in touch with him. His roommate had me worried when he told me that Terrell had left early that morning and never returned to the dorms. Terrell had a bad habit of disappearing when things got bad. I could never forget the time he lost his mother; he ran away from home. A week later, the police found him hanging on the corner with some drug dealers. At school, no one knew what to think about the situation.

As I lay in bed at 2:00 AM, I felt sorry for Terrell. He'd been through a lot in his life. There was only so much a person could take before they broke down. I prayed he stayed strong.

The second day I called for Terrell, he was still missing. His roommate seemed high, while I tried to get to the bottom of things. He was slurring and acting amused. I hung up in his face. I was tempted to mention the situation to Miss Sheila, but I didn't want to elevate her blood pressure when she'd been battling to keep it down. My blood pressure was probably high too. I'd been worrying myself to death. Last night my eyes couldn't stay closed; I was too worried about Terrell. He and Andrea had me stressed.

⌘　⌘　⌘

Late that evening, Terrell called me. Immediately, my stress level dropped. I was shocked when he asked me to pick him up from the airport. I hopped in my car and sped to Miami International Airport. When I got there, Terrell was standing outside. I was excited to see him. He threw a small suitcase in the trunk and got in the car. He hadn't been gone long, but he looked different. His perfectly trimmed goatee made him look mature. He hugged me and gave me a peck on the cheek.

"Wow, you look good," I said.

He rubbed his fingers down his neatly trimmed sideburns. "Thank you," he grinned.

"I see California's been good to you."

"Cali is nice but there's no place like home." Terrell tried handing me $20 for gas.

I pretended as if I didn't need it. "That's okay."

"You may not need it, but this car does," he said, peeking at the gas needle. "You need to stop acting like you don't need anybody."

I stopped acting stubborn and accepted the money. "Thank you."

"Don't sweat it."

I stopped at a gas station. Terrell got out, filled up my tank, and then went inside, bringing back a bag full of goodies.

"Have you decided if you're gonna go to school?" he said, handing me a Snapple.

"No."

"Real talk, I think you should go and do your thing. For real, yo," he said, smacking on his Cheetos.

I rolled my eyes to the ceiling. "I don't want to go to school."

"You don't have to go, but personally I think you have a lot to offer the world. I see you as a successful black woman, like the women on that show *Girlfriends*. They're beautiful, educated, and strong-minded. There's nothin' sexier than a sister who's got it going on."

"College doesn't make you brighter than anybody else. I know plenty of dummies that have graduated."

"I didn't say it did, but if you got the opportunity to go, then why not go?"

"Anyways, how do you like USC?"

"It's cool. I'm lovin' all the attention."

"I bet you are. You lucky dog."

"Coach said I'm gonna start this year."

I smiled. "Good for you."

"Yeah, I'm happy — but I'll be happier if you make that trip to Atlanta."

"My mind is already made up. I'm not leaving without Andrea."

Terrell sat quiet, shaking his head.

⌘　⌘　⌘

Terrell and I were in the front room looking at pictures when someone knocked at the door. Terrell opened the door and looked at me, surprised. Daddy walked in and stood at the door, looking around. Terrell looked embarrassed as he pulled up his jeans and grabbed his T-shirt off the couch. "I'll let you two be alone," he said, walking to his bedroom.

After Terrell left the room, Daddy looked at me. "I just dropped by to see how you were doing since I was in the neighborhood," he said.

"I'm fine."

"That's all I wanted to hear." He looked around again. "So where are you working?"

"At a major state-of-the-art call center. The pay and benefits are great. I'm looking forward to a management position." I felt bad for lying.

"That's what life is all about, doing the things that make you happy. My father despised my decision to become a police officer and look at me now. I'm the Chief of Police." My father opened the door. "Come over here and give me a hug before I go."

I stood up and gave my daddy a big hug.

"Take care of yourself," he said, walking out the door.

"Yes, sir." I wanted to grab him at the legs and beg him not to leave me. I couldn't believe he walked out the door without asking me to come back home. I watched him leave the parking lot. I felt like an idiot for lying to him, but I couldn't tell him that I didn't have a job.

Terrell walked out of his bedroom, pants sagging. "Is everything a'ight?" he said.

I was tired of him walking around half-naked, teasing me. "No, everything isn't all right." I put a hand on my hip. "I can't believe he didn't ask me to come back home."

"Remember, you're the one that left home."

"You have a good point."

"Please go home," he pleaded.

Please go put on a shirt, I wanted to say. "I'm not going any-where," I said, folding my arms stubbornly.

Terrell walked over to me and set his hands on my shoulders. "Do it for me," he said, kissing my forehead.

Automatically, my juices started flowing. I wanted to wrap my legs around his waist and give it to him.

"You deserve to be happy," he said.

I moved his hands off my shoulders and walked away before we ended up doing something we'd regret.

⌘　⌘　⌘

The next morning, we drove to the hospital. Terrell seemed uneasy. I couldn't blame him. Not only was he expecting his first child, but he also had to deal with Andrea's folks being at his throat. They'd lost their religion and resorted to pure hatred.

When we arrived at the hospital, Terrell wouldn't get out of the car. "What's the problem?" I said.

"You go ahead, man. I'll wait out here in the car."

"I'm not going to let you sit out here in the hot car."

"Trust me, I'm better off out here than up there with her crazy peoples."

I turned off the ignition. "Don't let her family intimidate you. There's something at this hospital that belongs to you. You'd be crazy to let them take it away."

Terrell opened the door and stepped out. "Let's go," he said. "You better have my back if they start trippin'."

Terrell and I stopped at the gift shop. He bought Andrea a card and balloons. I was proud of him for stepping up to the plate like a man, regardless of the odds against him. While God was molding good men, Terrell had to be the first in line. As we took the elevator upstairs, he closed his eyes. I took it that he was praying for strength.

As soon as we walked inside of the room, Andrea's daddy looked at Terrell coldly. Her father looked as if he wanted to spit in his face. He wasn't the only one. Andrea's mother, grandmother, uncle, and two cousins gave him a cold stare too. They acted as if he were the devil in flesh. I prayed Terrell wouldn't let their evil stares intimidate him.

"Why are you here? Haven't you've already done enough?" Andrea's daddy yelled.

Terrell sucked his teeth and that lit a fire. Andrea's daddy rose up out of his chair and rushed at Terrell. He grabbed Terrell's throat and shoved him against the wall. It took everybody in the room to get him off of Terrell. Afterwards, Terrell stormed out of the room. I chased him down the hall.

He stopped and snapped at me. "What, Karla?"

"Don't get snappy with me," I said.

He looked at me, chest heaved up. "I'm not in the mood for your li'l pep talks!"

"Excuse me then." I moved out of his way. I didn't think Terrell would hit a girl, but I didn't want to press my luck. He bumped my shoulder as he headed inside of the elevator, huffing and puffing. I went back to the room and told everyone goodbye. I wanted to stay at Andrea's side, but there were too many tempers in the room.

When I got downstairs to my car, Terrell wasn't anywhere in sight. I circled the hospital for an hour searching for him. I began to think I shouldn't have forced him to the hospital. A no-show would've been better than watching a *Jerry Springer* episode pop off inside of Andrea's room.

⌘　⌘　⌘

When I got home, Terrell wasn't at the crib. Usually, his shoes would be at the door. I refused to worry myself sick over him; I had enough problems of my own. I dropped on the couch and slept like a baby. When I woke up, Terrell was sitting at the end of the couch.

He looked at me. "You don't mind if I turn the TV, do you?" he said.

I nodded.

Terrell turned the television to the Raiders-Patriots pre-season game. He got excited. "Hot dog!" he said. "My dawg Randy Moss must be in a zone."

I went in the kitchen and started reading a book sitting on the table entitled *Invisible Man* by Ralph Ellison. I was five pages into the book when Terrell came in the kitchen. He made a lot of racket while making a grilled cheese. I went outside on the porch and picked up where I'd left off. For the first time since I'd moved to the hood, it was peaceful. It felt good knowing that the sun shone in the ghetto; the children were playing and the thugs were at ease instead of causing havoc on the block. I got distracted when Terrell came outside shirtless. I took a deep breath and continued reading.

He sat in the chair beside me. "I ain't mean to spazz out on you like that at the hospital," he said.

"I accept your apology."

"It's that simple, huh?"

"Yes."

He leaned over and pulled me into his strong arms. "See, that's why you my girl," he said, pecking me on the lips.

I got up because he'd crossed the line.

"Don't leave. I didn't mean to kiss you on the lips. The last thing I wanna do is make you feel uncomfortable."

I sat back down.

He started twiddling his thumbs. "I think I'm gonna go ahead and take that flight outta here tomorrow."

"I can't stop you, but I think you're making a big mistake."

"I mean, what can I do at this point? It's not like I haven't tried to be there for my unborn child."

"You can't be so quick to give up."

"Do you know how much strength it took me not to swing back at her pops? My own father ain't never put his hands on me. You talk a good game, but what about you?"

"What about me?"

"You're stubborn. There's no reason why you shouldn't be able to work things out with your folks. Life is too short for all the drama."

"My situation's different," I said.

"No it isn't. The bottom line is that we both got issues that need to be resolved." Terrell looked me in the eye and said, "Let's make a deal. I think if we both care about each other, we'll take the risk. Remember, we almost did on the beach."

"Don't remind me, please," I said, embarrassed.

He frowned. "Heck, I enjoyed it. I'm not gon' lie. Are you down or what?"

"What are you talking about?"

"If you go to Atlanta then I'll leave this weekend instead of tomorrow. Hopefully, she'll be done had the baby."

"I'm not leaving Andrea."

"You still gotta live your life, Karla. Look at me — I lost my mother, but I knew in my heart that she wanted me to keep goin'. So here I am, the first person in my family to go to college."

I gave him a hug. "Okay, I'll think about."

"You don't have much time, señorita. My flight leaves out at seven."

"On second thought, I'll go."

He smiled. "You won't regret it, Karla."

⌘   ⌘   ⌘

Early the next morning, I got up and drove home. As I stood at the door, I was hesitant to use my key. My eyes grew big when someone turned the door handle. I crossed my fingers, hoping Daddy would appear on the other side. Instead, it was my mother walking out the door for work. I wanted to shrink.

"Good morning," she said, looking surprised.

I was glad that she broke the ice. "Hi," I said.

Daddy trailed her out of the house. He looked at me and smiled. "Nice of you to drop in."

They left the door open for me. I thanked God, as they both hurried to their cars. I could tell they had a quickie because they both had pep to their step. As they were leaving, I rushed out to the driveway and stopped them.

"What is it?" Daddy said.

Both of my parents stared at me from inside their cars.

I put away my pride and said, "I'm sorry. I want to go to school . . . and, Mommy, I love you and Daddy so much."

My mother stepped out of her car and hugged me. "We love you too, and we want you to go to school."

Daddy winked at me and shouted, "Thank heavens!"

⌘   ⌘   ⌘

A day later, Mommy took me last-minute school shopping. She and Daddy made sure that I had everything I needed for my first semester at Spelman. Second semester, they told me I had to get a job. I didn't make a fuss. I'd planned on working anyway. I was excited beyond imagination. Then reality hit me when I got home and packed my things. Suddenly, the excitement turned into sorrow, because I was leaving tomorrow. My room looked empty. The only thing left in my closet was an old dusty yearbook full of memories. I was sad, but I felt as though I was ready to start a new chapter in my life.

That night, Terrell and I stayed on the phone for hours. Although we were tired, we remained on the phone because we weren't ready to tell each other goodbye.

The following morning, Mommy woke me up and made breakfast. Her salmon steak and grits was the bomb. I knew that I was going to miss her home cooking. After breakfast, Daddy packed my things into the car. I got teary-eyed as I watched him from my bedroom window.

Thirty minutes later, my mother called for me. I walked out of my bedroom admiring the posters of Usher hanging on the walls. As I closed the bedroom door, my phone started ringing.

"Karla baby, we're waiting on you!" my mother shouted again.

"Coming!" I shouted. Then I dived across my bed and picked up the phone.

"I'm glad I caught you," Terrell said. "You have to come to the hospital!"

"Why, what happened?"

"I can't talk right now." His voice trembled.

"You're scaring me. What's going on?"

"Just get your behind out here, girl." He hung up on me.

I rushed outside and begged my folks to take me to the hospital before we got on the road.

"Baby, we're already pressed for time," my mother said.

"Mommy, please," I begged. "I think something happened to Andrea!"

"All right," Daddy said.

I was worried to death. "Hurry, let's go!"

Daddy pushed the pedal to the metal.

⌘　⌘　⌘

When we got to the hospital, I didn't wait for my folks. I gave them the room number, and then ran inside. The elevator wouldn't move fast enough for me. As soon as it stopped, I ran to Andrea's room. I saw Terrell holding a baby wrapped in a blue blanket.

He looked at me and smiled, "It's a boy!"

My mouth dropped open. I had to pinch myself to make sure I wasn't dreaming.

"It's real, girl," he said.

I looked at Andrea's mother sitting in the corner. "Hi," I said. Then I looked at the baby, which was handsome like Terrell. I couldn't believe it.

The nurse came and took the baby. Terrell didn't want to let go of his son.

"What's the baby's name?" I said.

"We haven't thought of one yet," he said.

"Do you have any suggestions?" Andrea's mother asked me.

"No, but I'll come up with one. Where's Andrea?" I said, worried.

"The doctor had to run a few tests to make sure everything is normal. She opened her eyes this morning."

"It's a miracle!" I cried tears of joy.

"I want to thank both of you for all your cards and prayers," she said.

I walked over and hugged her. "You're welcome."

I was disappointed that I couldn't stay as long as I wanted to; I wanted to at least get the opportunity to see Andrea and hold the baby. Although I didn't get my wish, I was satisfied knowing they were all right.

Terrell followed me out of the room and squeezed me tight. "Y'all be safe on the road, Karla."

"Yes, sir."

"Watch out for the hound dogs up there. You know they like tender fresh meat."

I smiled. "I'll be fine."

"I know you'll hold it down. You too smart to let them cats run game on you."

"You be a good boy and don't get sidetracked out in Cali."

"Believe me, I won't. I have a son to keep me in check."

I heard my parents' voices from down the hall. I knew they were coming to get me. I gave Terrell a hug goodbye.

He acted like he didn't want to let me go.

"All right, Terrell, I get the point," I said.

My parents hit the corner while he held me hostage in his arms.

"I can't let you go, girl," he breathed deeply.

My daddy tapped him on the shoulder. "You need some help?"

Terrell almost jumped out of his britches. "No, sir," he said.

Daddy shook his hand and patted him on the back. "I'll let you slide even though you chose the Trojans."

"I'm sorry," he said.

Daddy laughed and walked away.

"Come on, sweetie," Mommy said, following him.

"Coming," I said.

Terrell looked at me. "Be safe."

"I will."

As I walked down the hall, I felt him watching me. When I turned around, he waved goodbye. Instead of waving, I blew him a kiss as I stepped in the elevator.

Clary Ingram would like to hear from you! You may contact this author at: writeclaryingram@gmail.com